Brannon leaned fo
seductive.

"Why not take this opportunity to—" Brannon ran his fingers up her arm "—explore?"

Addi's bright blue eyes darkened enticingly. Her lips parted but no sound came out.

Now that he'd voiced his idea out loud, Bran couldn't escape what a damn good idea it was. "Did you like kissing me, Addison?"

"I wasn't expecting it."

He raised his eyebrows. "That wasn't an answer."

She couldn't hold his gaze when she told him the truth. "I— Yes, of course."

He felt proud...and wary.

If *like* turned into more, then they weren't so much playing with fire as they were tossing a live grenade back and forth.

But he wanted more kisses. He wanted to earn his way into her bed this weekend.

* * *

One Wild Kiss by Jessica Lemmon is part of the Kiss and Tell series.

Dear Reader,

Is there any worse heart pain than having a crush on someone who doesn't like you back? Longing for someone who has no idea how you feel about them is the ultimate insult and injury! When we meet our beloved heroine, Addison, we learn she is suffering from a yearlong crush on *her boss*.

So inconvenient.

The Kiss and Tell series continues with the other Knox brother, Brannon Knox, whom you met in *His Forbidden Kiss*. At the time, he was planning to propose to the woman he was dating, but those plans were flipped upside down. Now that he's moved on, he's decided rather than focus on work, he's going to *play*. At the same time, Addison vows to be more practical and get over Brannon for good.

This book is a roller-coaster ride. There are twists, turns, ups, downs, and just when you think you have a handle on these two, one of them throws you for a loop! I hope you enjoy reading about Brannon and Addison. I also hope that if you are crushing on someone right now, they suddenly notice your affections, and the two of you live happily-ever-after. :)

Happy reading!

Jessica

PS: Craving more? You can find a printable book list, behind-the-scenes book secrets and blogs about writing at www.jessicalemmon.com.

JESSICA LEMMON

ONE WILD KISS

HARLEQUIN

DESIRE

HARLEQUIN®

DESIRE™

Recycling programs
for this product may
not exist in your area.

ISBN-13: 978-1-335-20904-7

One Wild Kiss

Copyright © 2020 by Jessica Lemmon

All rights reserved. No part of this book may be used or reproduced in
any manner whatsoever without written permission except in the case of
brief quotations embodied in critical articles and reviews.

This is a work of fiction. Names, characters, places and incidents
are either the product of the author's imagination or are used fictitiously.
Any resemblance to actual persons, living or dead, businesses,
companies, events or locales is entirely coincidental.

This edition published by arrangement with Harlequin Books S.A.

For questions and comments about the quality of this book,
please contact us at CustomerService@Harlequin.com.

Harlequin Enterprises ULC
22 Adelaide St. West, 40th Floor
Toronto, Ontario M5H 4E3, Canada
www.Harlequin.com

Printed in U.S.A.

A former job-hopper, **Jessica Lemmon** resides in Ohio with her husband and rescue dog. She holds a degree in graphic design currently gathering dust in an impressive frame. When she's not writing supersexy heroes, she can be found cooking, drawing, drinking coffee (okay, wine) and eating potato chips. She firmly believes God gifts us with talents for a purpose, and with His help, you can create the life you want.

Jessica is a social media junkie who loves to hear from readers. You can learn more at jessicalemmon.com.

Books by Jessica Lemmon

Harlequin Desire

Dallas Billionaires Club

Lone Star Lovers
A Snowbound Scandal
A Christmas Proposition

Kiss and Tell

His Forbidden Kiss
One Wild Kiss

Visit her Author Profile page at Harlequin.com, or jessicalemmon.com, for more titles.

You can also find Jessica Lemmon on Facebook, along with other Harlequin Desire authors, at Facebook.com/harlequindesireauthors!

For John.

I'll never forget the moment you called me out by asking, "Are you flirting with me?"

Why, yes. Yes, I was. ;)

One

Breathe in. Breathe out. He's just a guy.

Just a devastatingly handsome guy wearing an impeccably tailored navy designer suit.

Just a guy whose eyes were the color of bourbon enjoyed fireside.

Just a distractingly gorgeous guy whose hair was the perfect rumpled pattern of his own fingertips—or maybe some lucky woman's.

Just a guy who'd taken up residence in her heart and mind and soul for the past year who also happened to be her boss so he was Off Limits.

He's just a guy.

Addison Abrams started each of her workdays reciting that mantra before stepping into the ThomKnox building, entering the glass-walled elevator and zooming to the top floor of the multibillion-dollar tech company where her office was located.

When she accepted the position of executive assistant for the president of the company one year ago today, she'd expected said president to be older. Much older. Not six months older than her and closely resembling a model on the cover of *GQ* magazine. Granted, she hadn't done a ton of research on who she'd be working for. She saw the opportunity to work for a higher-up at ThomKnox and sent in her résumé so fast her own head had spun.

"I couldn't resist," that guy said now, setting a lone cupcake—vanilla with buttercream frosting, her favorite—in front of her. He lit a single gold candle with a match and then shook out the flame. She followed that trickle of smoke up to the face she saw every weekday. Once again, his sheer male beauty floored her. Seemed unfair to every other man on the planet that this one was hogging the good genes.

"Should I sing 'For She's a Jolly Good Executive Assistant' or 'Happy Workiversary to You'?" Brannon Knox gave her a wide smile, which disarmed her completely.

She'd been trying—fruitlessly—to stop admiring him, to stop longing for him, to stop looking at him like she wanted to take a bite out of him, for goodness' sake. Thank God for her poker face, because she hadn't yet been successful at getting over the crush she'd been harboring since the moment he extended his hand in greeting during her final interview.

Hi, I'm Brannon Knox. You can call me Bran.

"Singing is below your pay grade." She bent forward and gently blew out the flame. "This was unnecessary, but I appreciate it. Thank you."

Brannon Knox wasn't only the most beautiful man she'd ever laid eyes on, he was also kind and ruthlessly intelligent. Funny, tall, charming…and damned sexy. As if she hadn't thought about that enough already.

"I'm lucky to have you." He shoved his hands into the pants pockets of his suit and glanced over his shoulder as if making sure they were alone. "I should have thrown a big party, but I'm hopeless at doing anything without you." He winked, and even sitting, she felt her knees grow weak. Oh, how she wished that was true. That he needed her in other rooms besides the boardroom.

Like the bedroom. *Yum.*

"I'm happy to hear I'm indispensable." Practice made it possible for her to keep her smile cool and her fidgeting to a minimum. The throbbing heat working its way from her chest to her lap was the hardest to ignore, but she was doing her best. She'd convinced herself she couldn't help her physical reaction to him, since looking at Bran and wanting him came hand in hand.

But recently, she'd had a wake-up call. Her mind was made up. Even if her body was slower on the uptake.

"I'd give you the day off if we didn't have ten million things to do." His brow crinkled. "What am I doing today, anyway?"

She rattled off his schedule from memory: a conference call and two meetings.

"Plenty of time to grab a cup of coffee before the

day starts." Once again, he peeked over his shoulder. "I don't see any sign of the big bad CEO. Let's get out of here."

The *big bad CEO* was Bran's older brother, Royce Knox. A few months ago, Royce and Bran had both been contenders for the position when their father retired. Bran insisted that Royce won out because he was older, and she supposed that was true. Bran was amazing at what he did and every bit as capable as his older brother. In her eyes, he was the obvious number one choice for everything.

Once CEO, Royce had received more exciting news. He was going to be a father. The mother of his child, Taylor Thompson, was ThomKnox's COO—better known as a childhood friend to the Knoxes and the woman Bran used to *date*.

True story.

Addi had behaved like a jealous girlfriend during the short time Bran and Taylor dated. Though "dated" could be in quotation marks for as tepid as the romance had been. She would lay money on the fact that those two had never shared more than a kiss—though she'd never seen them kissing, either.

That unbecoming version of Addi was the old her. She was moving on with her life—disassembling the crush she had on Bran one swoony sigh at a time. She had to. Her job was important. Her pride was important. She wouldn't spend another moment longing for a guy who was uninterested in her.

"Coffee sounds amazing, but I really should return these emails." Best to keep work at work. They spent a lot of one-on-one time together discussing schedules and pertinent business information—a given for an executive assistant—but whenever she'd seen Bran outside these walls she began thinking of him as accessible. And, as she'd recently learned, he *wasn't* accessible. At least not to her.

"Come on, Addi." He leaned both hands on her desk, his jauntily patterned tie dangling between them. When he added an entrancing "let me take you out of here," she caved.

Old habits died hard.

"Fine, but I want an extra shot of espresso and two extra pumps of vanilla syrup." She pulled her purse from the bottom drawer of her desk and slung it over her shoulder. "And whipped cream on top."

He leaned in, his cunning smile further scrambling her brains, and added, "For your ThomKnox birthday, Addi, you can have anything on top you like."

Like you?

His innocent comment flooded her sex-starved body in a tidal wave and washed her all the way back to square one. This was going to be harder to do than she'd originally believed.

Her recent wake-up call had come courtesy of Bran's ex-girlfriend, Taylor. She'd innocently suggested that Brannon and Addison would "look good together," which meant Taylor noticed Addi's crush on him. The worst moment of Addi's life wasn't when she realized that Bran had overheard Taylor's matchmaking comment. It was the moment he'd reacted. In the long corridor bisecting the copy room, his face went slack, his expression pained.

Addison had wanted to die.

He might as well have held up a sign in all caps that read I DON'T FEEL THAT WAY ABOUT YOU, ADDISON. A sign she'd overlooked for way, *way* too long.

And since she loved her job and wanted to preserve what was left of her pride, burying her feelings was the wisest course of action. She'd had years of practice being independent. All she had to do was apply that same principle to her heart.

Tricky.

But necessary. If she had learned one thing from her parents, and it very well might be the only thing, it was that she couldn't rely on anyone else for anything. Not money, not friendship and certainly not love. A fact she'd forgotten as soon as she'd laid eyes on the younger Knox brother. A fact she was going to pound into her head with a sledgehammer if she had to—whatever it took to survive the travesty of a grown-up crush.

Maybe having coffee with Brannon would be a good thing. Platonic coworkers had coffee together all the time. And reaching the lower echelon of platonic coworkers was the goal. Not a very exciting goal, but she'd had enough excitement for a while.

"Get over him," she murmured, digging through her purse for her cell phone.

"What was that?" Bran asked as they stepped outside.

"Oh, nothing." She smiled up at him and her heart squeezed. An organ she'd recently determined had not one ounce of common sense.

* * *

The awkwardness continues.

Ever since Bran had dated Taylor, broken it off with Taylor and learned Royce had been named CEO, his work life had been challenging. Addison Abrams seemed to be another domino that had been reduced to rubble.

His executive assistant was irreplaceable. A trusted confidante who always had his back. She'd fit in since day one and brought with her an ease and efficiency that had helped him excel in his role as president. If she left, he'd…

Well, he couldn't think about it without seeing a mushroom cloud in his mind's eye. The saying went that behind every successful man was a strong woman. He'd made the epic mistake of believing Taylor was that woman. Now, he saw it was Addi.

Lately his relationship with Addi had been strained, and that blame could be placed directly on one rogue comment from Taylor Thompson. He didn't know if it was Taylor being in love with Royce or if it was pregnancy hormones that had made her say it, but she'd suggested that Addi should be more than his assistant. That they'd be good together. He and Addi had locked eyes wearing matched expressions of panic. His stemming from complete shock and hers from what appeared to be fear. Seriously. It was like a scene right out of Hitchcock's *The Birds*.

Fresh off the grave error of dating Taylor in the race to win the CEO role, Bran was determined not to follow that mistake with another. But he could admit that since it'd happened, he'd started noticing Addison.

Like, *noticing*.

His plan with Taylor had been shortsighted. Misguided. But at least he could explain it away. He thought having her at his side would make him appear more CEO-worthy. See? Misguided. After a few awkward dates, he thought he'd better their chances by...proposing.

It made sense at the time. Now, he swiped his brow in relief that they hadn't slept together. That would have made family holidays really awkward.

So. How did that tie in with Addi?

On the tail of the CEO race ending with Royce holding the baton, on Taylor becoming pregnant with Bran's niece or nephew, Bran found himself at the office more. Paying attention to his assistant more. Addi, whether she was trying to smooth over the uncomfortable suggestion that they should date or simply trying to soothe his ego, had been in his space more than usual.

He'd noticed her poise and passion when she discussed even the blandest work topics. He'd noticed her legs, long and lithe, and wondered if she was a runner or if hers was a yoga body. He'd noticed that she brought takeout from a local restaurant frequently, and she stayed to work late when he did.

In short, he'd noticed she was *single*.

Taylor's suggestion had taken a foothold in his subconscious. He'd begun thinking of Addi regularly—and not professionally. Which had led to the disastrously uneasy exchange this morning. Unbelievably, the after-effect with her was proving harder to hurdle than the almost-proposal to Taylor a few months ago.

Today being Addi's one-year anniversary at Thom-Knox was significant. If he intended on keeping her around for another year, he had to fix what was broken. He wasn't sure if coffee and an anniversary cupcake would be enough to usher the pink elephant out of the room, but it was a good start.

Outside in the gorgeous California sunshine, the office building towering over the green lawns dotted with reaching palm trees and colorful flowers, they crossed to the coffee shop that was a permanent fixture on the ThomKnox property. The Gnarly Bean served the best coffee in the state—he was hooked.

"I love this place." Addison's lips curled into a smile that made her blue eyes sparkle. She was dressed in yellow, her fair hair swept back into a cute ponytail. It was impossible not to notice how gorgeous she was. He'd sort of noticed since the day he hired her. But he could compartmentalize. He'd been great at compartmentalizing before the CEO obsession.

He pulled on the sleek silver handle of the glass door and gestured for her to enter ahead of him, pausing to inhale in appreciation. Was there any better indulgence in life than coffee?

Automatically his eyes tracked to Addi's legs. *Just one.*

"I'm buying," he reminded her when she reached for her wallet. He could've sworn her bright blue eyes flicked to his mouth a second before her own beautiful lips formed the words "thank you." Probably he was projecting.

The worst part about what went down a few months ago was that he'd behaved so out of character he'd hardly recognized himself. He hadn't asked Taylor to date him because he was attracted to her, but because he'd hoped their partnership would make him a better contender. It was like an alien had taken over his body. Bran was the easygoing, playful Knox brother; robotic pragmatist described Royce.

"We should do this more often," Bran said.

She watched him carefully, her expression unreadable.

Oh-kay. Going well so far.

"Morning, Addi." The barista met her at the counter, smiling around a beard and subtly flexing the tattoos on his forearms.

Pathetic.

"Hey, Ken. How are you?" Addi greeted him warmly and Bran felt a twinge of jealousy. Beard and tattoos? Was that what she was into?

Suddenly he felt like a stodgy guy in a suit whose only importance was signing her paychecks. He never used to notice who Addi smiled at—until she stopped smiling at him. God, he missed the simplicity of the good ol' days. Back when he saw himself in the role of "boss" and her in the role of "assistant" and never the twain shall meet.

Before Taylor pointed out that they'd look good together.

Before Royce suggested the girl for Bran was right under his nose.

Before Bran starred in his own personal remake of *Invasion of the Body Snatchers*.

He used to live life day by day without worrying about the future. Those were the days.

Ken said something stupid and Addi laughed—surely to be polite. Bran stepped between them and Ken's smile turned challenging.

"She wants whipped cream on top, and I promised to give her whatever she wants. It's our one-year anniversary today. Isn't it, Ad?"

Her cheeks turned pink, but her smile was genuine and focused on Bran for a change.

"It is," she agreed.

"Congratulations," Ken said as he tapped the screen to add the upcharge. Bran didn't think he meant it.

And even though he was setting a course to win back the trust of his trusty executive assistant, he saw no harm in making sure that Ken, here, didn't tread where he wasn't welcome. Addi could do better than a hairy barista, anyway, so Bran had no problem reminding this guy of his station.

After all, what were bosses for if not to protect their most treasured coworkers?

Two

Addison was contemplating Bran's behavior at the Gnarly Bean yesterday when Taylor Thompson stepped into her office.

"Knock, knock. You should demand a door. Anyone could barge in." Taylor was referring to the dividing wall separating Addi from the rest of the office, and Bran's office, which was to the left of her desk.

"You are the COO. Barge away."

"Ugh. Let's stop talking about barges. I already feel like one." Taylor smoothed a hand over the small baby bump protruding from her black Dolce & Gabbana midi dress.

"Stop it. You look amazing. How's everything going?" Addi asked.

"Do you mean with work, the pregnancy, the engagement or moving in with Royce?" Taylor's eyes widened slightly. Her life had changed drastically over the last few months, so it must be hard to wrap her head around. It wasn't long ago that Addi had flipped the light switch on for the copy room and stumbled across Royce and Taylor making out in the supply closet.

Thank goodness those days were behind them. At the time she'd been so jealous of Taylor and Bran's relationship. Now Addi could hardly believe how immature she'd been. It was obvious Taylor had found her other half in Royce.

Addi had since apologized for being rude—while avoiding mentioning that it was because she was half in love with Bran—and because Taylor was at once charming and classy, she'd apologized right back and asked if they could be friends.

Taylor lowered into the guest chair in front of Addi's desk. "I've never been so busy and yet I feel like I'm exactly where I should be. Does that make sense?"

"Complete sense." Addi smiled. She used to believe she was exactly where she should be. Before Bran started acting weird around her. What was with that display with the barista yesterday morning, anyway? Ken and Bran seemed to be having some sort of modern-day Wild West standoff.

Men made no sense. Maybe it was time to stop trying to figure them out.

"It's incredible that I get anything done considering I can't have caffeine right now." Taylor grimaced.

"I'd die." Addi tucked her coffee mug behind her computer screen to hide it from view.

"That's the price of having a healthy son or daughter. It's strange not knowing what to call my baby. I can't very well say 'it,' can I?"

"You don't want to know the sex?" Addi didn't know if she could stand the suspense if she were pregnant.

"I do. And I don't. Everything about my and Royce's relationship has been a surprise. Why not surprise ourselves with a little girl or boy?" She rubbed her round tummy.

"I'm happy for you." Addi meant it. Taylor was glowing and not just from the pregnancy. Whenever she was with Royce, the other woman lit up like the northern lights. "Have you set a wedding date yet?"

"Ho boy." Taylor admired the gigantic diamond solitaire on her left hand. "I know the engagement will lead to a wedding, but we're not sure when. We're taking things a day at a time."

Unplanned pregnancy and closet kisses aside, Taylor had handled life's many curveballs with a grace Addi hoped one day to possess.

"Happy belated anniversary, by the way. I saw Bran with a pair of cupcakes yesterday."

"Funny. He only gave me one." Addi narrowed her eyes playfully, trying not to let any of her feelings for him show. Walking around half in love with him was not healthy—and behaving like a lovesick woman in front of Taylor was asking for it. "I'm lucky to work for people who care. I've had bosses who didn't."

A lot of them. She'd shunned her parents' money when she didn't follow their rules for her life. Seceding from the union five years ago to pave her own way had come at a price. There were a lot of ramen noodles in her past, and plenty of bills that had been paid late. But that was in her past. When she landed the position at ThomKnox, she knew she was in the right place. They paid her well, and the higher-ups actually cared. Jack Knox, Bran's dad, had always treated her with respect and addressed her warmly.

And recently she'd almost blown it. Over what? A schoolgirl crush? No more.

She would never go back to scraping by or working for companies that gladly stepped on the "little people" to pave their mansions' driveways with gold bars. The Knoxes—and Taylor would soon be one—were good people. Addi was a good person. And she was no longer going to let a silly attraction distract her from what was important.

"Now for the real reason I came here. When's Brannon back?" Taylor glanced at his dark office.

"He had an early meeting before work. He should be here soon." Addi glanced at the clock. "You're welcome to wait."

"No, that's okay. I'll track him down later." Taylor stood and seemed to quietly debate before asking, "Are you and Brannon…okay?"

"Of course!" Addi said a little too loudly. "Why wouldn't we be?"

"Come on, Ad. Just us girls here. I see the way you look at him."

Was she so transparent? "He's…very nice. But I'm not interested in him like that." *Starting right now.*

"That's too bad." Taylor's mouth quirked.

It really was.

"We're fantastic coworkers." It was such a dry, stale definition for how she felt about him, Addi internally cringed.

"Right." Taylor nodded but didn't look convinced. "Tell him I stopped by. And enjoy some of that coffee for me."

Addi watched Taylor go, her stomach pinching. That happened whenever she didn't tell the truth. She appeased her conscious with the reminder that soon, it would be true.

One day she'd be as immune to Bran as he was to her.

Three

When Taylor strolled by, Bran stepped out of the copy room and intercepted her path. He'd been en route to his own office when he'd heard her and Addi's conversation. He'd rerouted before his presence was known and made everything between him and his assistant worse. If that was possible.

"Bran, hey. I was just at your office."

"I know." He folded his arms over his chest. "I *heard*."

To her credit, Taylor winced. But she followed it up with a justification. "You can't blame me for trying!"

Gently, he gripped her biceps and towed her into the copy room where he closed the door. "You have to stop doing this."

"Doing what?"

"You can't make two people fall in love because

they're both good-looking." He lifted an eyebrow and complimented them both. "As well you know."

"Ha ha. And that's not the only reason."

Something was suspicious in the way she examined the floor.

"What's the *other* reason?"

"What do you mean?"

He knew her well enough to know that her innocence was one hundred percent feigned. *"Taylor."*

"I just…want you to be okay. I worry."

Ah, Taylor. She really was so sweet.

"About me?" he asked.

"Yes. You almost proposed to me, Brannon."

"A mistake."

"Obviously. But I would like to see you with a nice girl. And Addi likes you. I don't care what she says."

"A nice girl—Taylor, you're not my mother. You don't have to fix me up. And you should care what Addi says. You're freaking her out and I need her to keep this job or else I'll be demoted to the tech department with Cooper."

Jayson Cooper was Bran's ex-brother-in-law. Taylor chuckled, understanding that Bran was joking. Cooper and Bran's sister, Gia, worked side by side in the tech department. It was the heart of ThomKnox.

"You deserve to be happy. That's all I'm saying."

See? Sweet.

He touched her shoulder, grateful to have a friend who cared that much about him—even if it was slightly emasculating. "I'm in the process of putting everything back where it goes. I'm not jealous of Royce about CEO, or anything else." He gave her a meaningful look. "And dating Addi isn't going to help me be happier. If anything, it'll end badly and I'll be more alone than ever. You don't want me to hire an assistant like Royce's, do you?"

Melinda was an ace, but she was also sort of terrifying. As if reading his mind, Taylor shuddered. "*No.* Let's keep Addi."

"Yes, let's." He opened the copy room door. "Now what was it that you wanted to talk to me about? Should we grab a conference room?"

"Actually I'm starving." She patted her belly. "How about we grab a snack?"

"We can do that," he told her and they walked to the elevator. "And just so we're clear…"

Taylor turned, wide-eyed innocence worn like a mask.

"Addi and I are trying to make our way back to professional coworkers after you kicked open the 'Bran + Addi' door. Can you do me a favor and let us close it?"

She sighed, her shoulders slouching in her designer dress. "*Fine.* But I won't like it."

He pressed the button for the elevator and smiled. "I'm sure you won't."

After his impromptu breakfast with Taylor, Bran strolled toward his office. He came to an abrupt halt when he saw Addi scrambling in the lap drawer of her desk for a tissue, fresh tears wetting her cheeks. She pasted on a smile that wasn't the least bit sincere.

"Hey," he said, unsure what else to say.

He had a mother. He had a sister. Seeing either of

them in tears made him feel two things: helpless…and helpless. He felt the same way now.

"Morning," she said. "How was the meeting with Frank?"

He could pretend not to notice. Save her the embarrassment. But what kind of jerk would he be if he did that? His goal was to keep her from leaving and if her tears had to do with something he could help with professionally he needed to know about it.

"The meeting went well. I ran into Taylor on the way back."

"Oh good. She was looking for you." Addi blinked damp eyes at him, but she didn't appear to be reeling from Taylor's visit.

No, Addi's eyes were filled with sadness. Something had broken her heart. Or someone. Did he guess wrong about her being single? Did she have a boyfriend she never talked about?

He lowered himself onto the corner of her desk, catching sight of cream-colored card stock and a black envelope. Fancy. The kind of paper used for—

"A wedding?" he guessed.

Those sad blue eyes turned up to his, her expression both startled and vulnerable.

"The invitation," he clarified. "Weddings aren't always good news." Especially if, for example, the groom was her ex.

"Oh, um, no. It's a family…reunion." She stuffed the invitation into her planner. Formal for a family reunion, but okay.

"Everything all right?" he asked gently.

"Yes! Completely fine." Her smile was shaky. "Family can be tricky."

"Try working with them every day."

Her smile was genuine this time and made this awkward interchange worth it in every way. "I couldn't walk by and pretend not to notice. I'm not that obtuse."

"Ha!" She slapped her hand over her smile, then waved the air in front of her. "I'm sorry. Ignore me. I'm fine. Honestly."

Against his better judgment, he captured her smaller hand in his. "You're human. It's okay to cry."

Warmth between their palms radiated up his arm, attraction snapping the air between them like a leashed alligator. Meanwhile, Addi regarded him like he *was* a leashed alligator.

He gave her hand a squeeze before dropping it and standing from her desk. "If you need to take off—"

"No. Thank you." Her tears had dried already, her smile glued into place.

"Don't say I didn't offer." He pointed at his office door. "You know where to find me."

He shut himself inside and sat in his chair, eyeing the Post-it stuck to his laptop that read, *Taylor stopped by. Not urgent.* Addi's handwriting was pretty and delicate, like she'd been a moment ago. Whatever family thing was going on—if that was the truth—he didn't like how it'd affected her.

His cell phone buzzed with a reply to his earlier text to Tammie. When he'd sent it, he wasn't sure if he was hoping she'd reply or hoping she wouldn't. Similarly, he wasn't sure whether or not to read it.

He grabbed his cell phone anyway, too curious to ignore her reply.

Been a while.

A long-ass while.

In an effort to put everything back to normal, there was one issue to contend with that he hadn't talked about with anyone.

His roving libido.

He hadn't had a woman in his bed in a long time and had become suddenly distracted by Addison Abrams. Which was detrimental to the balance he was trying to restore at the office.

This morning, the *situation* had escalated. He'd woken hard and ready, unable to think of anything but sex. Sex with Addison.

He blamed the dry spell that had yet to end. From now on, his work and personal life had clear lines of demarcation. He needed to get laid, and obviously the best choice was to find someone outside of work to satisfy that urge.

The simplest fix was a sure thing by the name of Tammie. He'd sent her a text after a, um, *rejuvenating* shower, inviting her out for drinks.

Too long, he typed.

Her reply lit the screen half a second later. Thursday at 7? Vive?

Vive was a dark, classy bar with rich red velvet on the booth seats and cozy, sexy nooks filled with shadows.

Perfect. Meet you there.

He tossed his phone on his desk. Sex with Tammie would fix more than his blue balls. Sex with Tammie was a time machine back to before the whole "who will be named CEO" fiasco. Back when he knew how to lighten up. Back when "work hard, play hard" was his motto. Hell, this year all he'd done was work hard and then work *harder*.

Was it any wonder Addi had followed him around, staying late to make sure he was okay?

He glanced out his window at her. She was typing on her keyboard, her attention fixed on her computer screen. The pull he felt toward her, the concern he had for her, was alive and well, but he wouldn't allow it to harm their friendship or their working relationship.

She deserved to feel comfortable at work and he didn't need her—or Taylor—worrying about him. What he needed was to focus his physical attention on a woman who wouldn't worry about him for longer than one night.

His phone buzzed with another text from Tammie. A red lips emoji.

By Friday morning, this situation with Addi would be resolved.

I'm not that obtuse.

Addison hadn't meant to literally laugh out loud, but

come on. He'd been pretty darn obtuse! Not only had he bought her lie about a family reunion but he'd also completely missed the way she'd drooled over him for the last year.

Obtuse or not, him consoling her when she'd been crying had tugged at her heartstrings.

"Just when I decided to get over him," she mumbled to herself.

She reached for her cell phone to text her friend. Carey was out of the country traveling for work, but Addi needed to talk to someone, even if the conversation was one-way.

She texted, Just cried in front of my boss. Go me! and sat back in her chair, her eye catching the invitation in the inside pocket of her planner. The very card stock she'd been holding when Bran caught her crying.

Behind the paper was a black envelope on which her name and address had been meticulously scripted in gold ink. Grief weighed heavy on her chest.

Joe was too young to die.

The invitation had arrived yesterday but she'd neglected to check her mailbox until this morning. As a result, she'd shoved it into her planner and promptly forgotten about it. When she finally remembered and tore open the envelope, she was shocked to see that it contained an invitation to Joe's "celebration of life."

He'd passed away over a month ago and had been cremated per his wishes. According to his family, funeral plans were "forthcoming." Joe, as it turned out, had arranged those plans before he passed away. He'd selected a group of friends and family to attend an intimate but luxe party at a resort in Lake Tahoe. He'd covered the expenses for guest rooms and had prearranged an itinerary and catering. The lush surprise was so…him.

The last time she'd seen Joe had been around Christmas. It had broken her heart to see him so frail, and it'd broken his heart for her to see him that way, too. *Don't you dare come back here, Addi*, he'd told her. *I don't want you to remember me like this.*

She'd swallowed tears she'd promised not to shed while sitting next to him. They'd drifted apart—and hadn't hung out in years—but he'd meant a lot to her. Losing someone was hard. Losing someone she'd known and cared for as long as she'd known and cared for Joe had seemed insurmountable.

It wouldn't surprise her if that visit had been what turned up the volume on her crush on Bran. She'd mentioned her boss to Joe at the time, if only to change the subject. Joe had encouraged her to "go for it." But he had lived a big, brave life thanks to a family that was drowning in money and eagerly showered it on him. She'd reasoned it was easier to be brave when there was a few billion in the bank.

Receiving the invitation to his life celebration had brought the grief of that December day back in an instant. Addi was a private person. She reserved messy emotions for when she was alone. If Bran's attention hadn't been so welcome, she might've been embarrassed about carrying on like that at work.

She shut her eyes against the memory of how great

Bran had smelled sitting so close. Like mountain pine and citrus—

That's enough.

Operation Get Over Him was a new endeavor, but an important one. Focusing on her independence would fortify her job, which would keep her housed and well-fed, as well as heal her heart.

The upcoming trip to Lake Tahoe would bring closure to another wound in her past—she hadn't seen Joe's parents since she stopped working for Hart Media, and as a result royally pissed off her own parents. While a resolution with her parents was too much to count on, maybe the Harts would surprise her.

After a quick call to the inn where Joe's life celebration was being held, she learned that her room had been reserved, the cost covered. Travel was easy since the lake was a four-hour drive away. A trip even her questionably reliable car could handle.

Onward.

Satisfied that at least her personal life was moving forward, she jotted the trip into her planner. The only thing left to do was schedule her time out of the office and a temp to fill her chair for a few days.

A long weekend celebration was a perfect sendoff for Joe, and the perfect time to bury her crush on Brannon Knox.

Out of sight, out of mind and all that.

Four

In a traffic-clogged lane on the freeway, Addison worried her lip with her teeth as she watched a trail of smoke snake out from under the hood of her hatchback. She was no mechanic, but she guessed that smoke coming from any part of her car was *bad*.

She was twenty minutes into her trip with several hours to go. She just needed a little bit of luck. She shut off the air-conditioning, hoping that taking the AC out of the equation would encourage her antique car to complete its journey as far as the next exit, but her beloved rust bucket jerked forward one final time before wheezing and, ultimately, stalling.

Lady Luck had given her the finger.

Honks sounded in the air, along with a few choice swear words from her fellow commuters. Like she *de-*

cided to break down? She was tempted to shout back at them. Something to the effect of, "Oh, you know, just taking a breather here in the far right lane!" Instead she bit her tongue, grateful that she'd managed to steer onto the shoulder at least partially.

Her entire morning had been frustrating.

She'd forgotten to halt her mail and discovered this morning that the post office's website was down. So she'd physically driven to the post office and waited in line and then filled out one of those stupid forms. As a result, her planned departure from River Grove at 10:00 a.m. had been delayed two hours.

And now this.

Well. She was going to have to call for help.

Her parents weren't an option and hadn't been for some time. Discussion of a broken-down car would lead them to remind her how if she'd stayed "at Joe's family's company," she'd not only have reliable transportation but also would have funded her retirement by now. She guessed they still held her responsible for the fracture in their relationship with the Harts, but Addi refused to take the blame. She'd worked hard to get where she was in life. Her parents might not give her credit for thriving without their money or connections, but she was proud of herself.

She typed tow trucks Silicon Valley into her phone. Approximately six million options popped up on the screen. How was she supposed to know who was reliable? Who wouldn't overcharge her? Who would be the fastest?

She debated for the count of three drivers who sped

past and flipped her off before calling the most logical person. If there was a silver lining for this crappy day, it was that her car had chosen to croak ten miles from ThomKnox headquarters.

"Mr. Brannon Knox's office, may I help you?" answered the temp currently stationed at Addi's desk.

"Hi, this is Addison Abrams, Brannon's executive assistant. Is he available?"

"One moment."

A brief pause later, Bran's silky voice was caressing her ear canal. "Couldn't stay away, I see."

"My car broke down. I was hoping you could recommend a towing company." She rattled off the nearest exit and then had to repeat herself when some jerk swerved around her, horn blaring.

"What the hell was that? Are you okay?"

"Apparently it's frowned upon to have car trouble on the 80."

"You realize you could wait an hour or two for a tow truck to arrive, and that's optimistic."

She grunted. "That sounds about right for today."

"I'll pick you up myself."

He'd…what?

"Oh, no. I didn't mean for—"

"Addison." Those three sternly spoken syllables locked her throat. "Sit tight. I'm coming for you."

Congratulations! You've just unlocked another Brannon Knox fantasy badge.

Her car's hood was up, Bran's upper half hidden under it. His suit jacket was tossed over the front seat of his shiny red sports car, which he'd parked in front of her car and off to the side. A tow truck was on its way, but he'd insisted on having a look himself. Before this moment, she would've bet her life savings that Bran didn't have a clue about cars. Why would he? He was a billionaire. Everything was probably done *for* him.

But no, of course he knew enough to climb on in and make another of her sexual fantasies about him bloom to life. He pulled this wire and that, checked a dipstick here and twisted a cap there. All while she admired the ropey muscles of his forearms and the way his white shirt stuck to the muscles of his back thanks to a damp pool of sweat.

He cranked something or another, grunting with exertion while she silently lectured her lady parts. Him attempting to resuscitate a vehicle was hands down the sexiest thing she'd ever seen him do. There was no desk hiding his long legs, encased in charcoal trousers and leading up to a spectacular ass. She'd always admired Bran's backside, and now she could do it without worry of being caught.

She wrenched her eyes from his amazing physique to watch those hands twisting and tightening. The longer hair on top of his head fell over his forehead, sweat trickled down his face as he grimaced with effort. Her gaze wandered south of its own accord as she pictured him exerting himself elsewhere, same sweat, same hair on his forehead, only he'd be over top of her. Or beneath her.

Oh, yes.

"Well." He emerged from under the hood and she

jerked her attention from his butt. "Your radiator's shot. Probably more than the radiator, but that part I know for sure." There was an oil streak on his face and his hair was more rumpled than usual.

Sexxxxy.

The meager progress she'd made getting over him had suffered a major setback thanks to this circumstance. Heaven help her.

He dropped the hood with a bang and wiped his hands on what looked like an expensive pocket square. It was paisley—silk, she'd bet. Not to mention the shirt that stretched over his ample chest, covering three-quarters of those capable arms, was ruined as well.

"Your *wardrobe* is shot. You'll have to take it out of my paycheck."

He grinned and she nearly swooned on the side of the freeway. "Sounds like me. Help out a damsel in distress and then dock her pay. What kind of a guy would I be if I let you fend for yourself?"

"A practical one?"

Her reward was his husky laugh that made her ankles tremble. Interestingly enough, no one had yelled at her since Brannon arrived. It was as if they understood they were in the presence of power.

"Come on, I'll give you a ride to the office."

She retrieved her purse from her front seat while he transferred her luggage to the trunk of his incredibly shiny car.

"Is this new?" she asked as she sank into the butter-soft leather passenger seat. She could swear she'd never seen this car before.

"Very new. She's one day old. Had her delivered last night." He settled in the driver's seat, picked his moment and smoothly pulled into traffic. "I haven't been able to drive her anywhere but work, but I'm itching to take her out."

"I'll bet."

He put his foot on the gas and the engine growled, sending tingles through her feet and up her legs.

"You were headed to Tahoe, right?" he asked.

"Yeah."

"For a reunion."

He wasn't technically wrong, so she nodded. "How long do you think it'll take for my car to be repaired?"

"Hard to say. Depends on whether the mechanic has the parts he needs, and if he has five cars in front of yours or fifty."

Her shoulders sagged. That piece of crap car was her only means of transportation. And if repairing it cost more than the vehicle's worth—a probability—she'd have to go through the hassle of buying a new one.

"Why are you driving a car in that bad a shape, anyway? Tell me it's not because I don't pay you enough."

"No! Oh my gosh. Not at all." He took very good care of her in the money department. "It's… I keep it for sentimental reasons."

"Really?" His dubious expression said what he didn't. How could she be sentimental over such an ugly hunk of metal?

"That car was the first big purchase I made with my own money." She'd hunted countless dealerships and sifted through online classifieds. She'd taken care of the transaction herself. It'd been scary at first, but then enthralling. That was the day she knew that she didn't have to be scooped under her parents' wings to make it in life. That she was capable of surviving on her own.

Though she'd sort of been scooped up under Bran's wing today. It was past time to reclaim that plucky woman who had ventured off on her own. To be as independent as she'd once been.

"I remember my first car," he said wistfully.

"Was it a Maserati?"

"Maybe." He flashed her a quick smile and she had to laugh. "When do you need to arrive in Tahoe?"

"My reservations are for tonight."

"You should take a jet. You'd be there before you know it."

Sure. She'd just *charter a jet*.

"I don't fly. But thank you."

"You *don't* fly?" One judgmental eyebrow climbed his forehead.

"No. I *don't* fly. I like the wheels touching the road at all times during my commute." Feeling more and more like a problem he had to solve, she asked, "Can you drop me at a car rental place? There has to be one nearby."

She'd arrive later than she wanted—way later—but at least she'd be there.

"Why don't I take you?"

"What? No. I mean, no, thank you," she added, not wanting to sound ungrateful. "I wouldn't dream of putting you out."

"Did I not say I needed to take this car on a road trip? This is the perfect excuse for me to spend some time with her." He stroked the dashboard and gave the car a gentle pat. Then he slid Addi a wink and she melted into the interior.

"B-but you'll have to drive back. Won't you be tired?"

"I'll grab a room. Wouldn't hurt to have a night away. Maybe you can take a break from your family and grab a drink or dinner with me. It'll be fun."

Fun? She might die if she spent four-plus hours in the car with a winking, eyebrow-raising Brannon who had a smudge of oil on his cheek.

He slid over three lanes of traffic with barely any effort, ignoring a blaring car horn when he did. Pedal to the floor, he whipped around a truck and opened up the engine.

"Gotta love turbo," he said over the feral growl. "Give me ten minutes to change and pack and we'll be on our way." He slanted her a look, seeking permission. "Okay?"

"What about the office…"

"I'm a big boy. I can take off work to deliver my valuable assistant safely to Lake Tahoe. Unless you don't want to hang out with me." His tone was more of a dare than a question. "Am I skeevy? Is that it?"

"That's not it. Stop making fun of me!" She nudged his arm and felt the hard muscle there as he shifted gears. Touching him casually wasn't her norm. He felt like a solid wall. A very warm, solid wall. *Whew*. Was it hot in here? She fiddled with the vent and aimed the AC at her face.

"You're very hard to treat. I practically had to beg

to take you out for coffee on Monday morning. Now you're going to make me beg to let me drive you to Tahoe when the very thing you need and want most is travel to Tahoe?"

Oh trust me, that's not what I want most.

But she couldn't refuse him. This sexy billionaire with a healthy dash of confidence was her undoing.

"Say thank you, Addi."

"Thank you, Addi," she said with an eye roll.

"That's more like it." He adjusted the vent in front of her. "Better?"

The best. Watching his fingers press the temperature control nearly gave her an orgasm. She really needed to get out more.

"A-as long as you're sure I'm not interrupting any of your plans."

"Nah," he said as he weaved around a line of cars and angled for an exit. "I don't have any plans tonight."

Five

Nothing that can't be canceled, Bran amended.

His date with Tammie was tonight—something he'd remembered, oh, about thirty seconds ago. She'd forgive him. Probably.

Addi crossed her legs primly, one calf sliding over the other, one sexy wedge heel stacked on the other. In the tight confines of his new car, those legs looked a mile long. Long enough to make his breaths shorten and his mind wander. Was it any wonder she'd wiggled into his fantasies?

He'd gone back and forth deciding if she had a boyfriend, but this situation had given him the definitive no he'd suspected. If Ad was dating someone, she'd have called him, not Bran. And no decent guy would let her drive that rattletrap of a car, either. Unless she'd started dating the barista. Who knew what Ken would allow her to do? Bran wrinkled his nose.

Leaving Addison standing alone in the middle of the highway was not an option. She could be hit by an oncoming truck, or *hit on* by the tow truck driver. Anything could happen to a beautiful woman in the center of the freeway. He understood that she liked to rely on herself, a quality he respected. He had no problem with a strong woman. But she had to know when to let someone take care of her. Today he'd had the time, the means and the inclination to pick her up. He'd have done it for anyone.

But driving her to Tahoe? That wasn't something he'd have done for just anyone.

That was something he'd offered to do for Addi. *And why is that?*

Why didn't he arrange a rental car for her instead? Why didn't he talk her into taking the corporate jet? Why did he insist on delivering her personally to safety?

Because we're friends.

Because she's a valuable employee.

Because I want her to know she can count on me.

Damn.

He'd never thought of himself as having a white knight complex, but that last reason was a touch more honest than the other two. When he'd offered to drive her to Lake Tahoe, her shoulders had dropped from their position under her ears. Setting her at ease was enough, even if they never closed the chasm between them.

The offer of dinner tonight was as casual as the coffee the other day, he further defended. But it wouldn't stay that way if he kept eyeing her legs.

He was fairly certain he'd felt an answering sexual awareness the moment they settled into the bucket seats of his car. Despite her saying she wasn't interested in him, he'd felt that bolt of lightning when she'd touched him. He had a hard time believing that zap only went one way.

Regardless. He wasn't pursuing her. The two things he'd focus on during this road trip were not Addi's legs. That would be safe travels and the new girl in his life: his Misano Red Audi RS 7 Sportback.

There.

Now that he'd justified that half to death...

Twenty minutes later, he pulled into his driveway and parked. When she didn't get out behind him, he opened her door, narrowly avoiding eyeing those long legs again.

"I'll wait here," she said.

"You sure you don't want to come inside?"

"No. No, no, no." She'd turned him down—four times, no less—with a smile.

"I'll be quick."

"Okay." She pulled out her cell phone and began scrolling, busying herself with something other than a tour of his place. Maybe it was inappropriate to invite her into his house since she'd never been here before.

When he'd hired one Miss Addison Abrams, he'd been pleased when she lived up to her résumé. Her work record was impressive. She'd been employed for several large companies and understood corporate regimens.

She interviewed well, too. She was confident, poised and beautiful. Which he wasn't supposed to take into account, but her attributes were impossible to dismiss.

Bran never considered himself to have a "type" but he did love a California girl, and Addi was golden, blue-eyed and blonde. His weakness.

"Well, you're going to have to be strong," he reminded himself as he stuffed clothes into a bag. He'd done a fine job of compartmentalizing her until recently. Damn Taylor.

He changed from his suit pants and oil-streaked button-down into jeans and a T-shirt and tied his sneakers. At the last second, he grabbed a fresh suit, too, in case dinner was formal.

He jogged downstairs with his bag, excited at the prospect of taking a break. Hell, if tonight went well, maybe he'd stay the weekend. He'd felt no such excitement about meeting Tammie at Vive. Which reminded him...

He texted Tammie a quick message: Have to cancel tonight. Something came up. By the time he'd locked his front door and was sliding into the car next to Addi, he'd almost forgotten he'd sent it. Leaned back in the passenger seat of his car, her blond ponytail blowing in the breeze, her elbow resting on the window's edge... She looked damn good in his car. Any guy who caught sight of her looking this tempting would forget his own name.

His phone buzzed from its resting spot on the gear box and Addi's eyes went to it at the same time his did.

A photo of Tammie's low-cut top and plentiful cleavage flashed onto the screen.

"Shit." He picked up his phone. "Sorry about that."

"No judgment here." She held up a hand.

Beneath the lewd photo, the text read, Can I change your mind?

He replied, Going out of town. Rain check.

We'll see came Tammie's reply.

He shook his head. Not because he'd messed up his "sure thing" but because he didn't remotely care about seeing her once he was back home. What had he been thinking? That the attraction he felt for Addi could be painted over with a girl like Tammie? Impossible.

Not the point. He wasn't pursuing Addi.

"I didn't peg you for a clean lines kind of guy," his adorable assistant said, her eyes on his house and, he noticed, not on his phone.

"I don't like clutter."

She hummed but didn't look at him. He had an idea how to get her attention, even if it was a tad immature.

"Sorry you can't go topless."

He earned a wide-eyed look of surprise.

"I almost bought a convertible, but I couldn't resist the sleekness of this model. Was that joke too soon?"

She held her finger and thumb an inch apart and peered at him through the gap. So damn cute.

"Windows down okay?" He pressed a button and both driver's and passenger's windows lowered. "Some women don't want to mess up their hair."

"Like the woman on your phone?"

"Oh-ho! I sense a little bit of judgment." He mirrored

her earlier gesture and held his own finger and thumb an inch apart. "I canceled my date with her tonight. I guess that was her way of trying to change my mind."

"That lacks creativity." Addi tilted her head and a flirty smile crossed her lips. He could feel them sliding back into the comfortable groove they'd worn in at the office.

The only new part was that the joking was starting to feel a lot like flirting.

An excited glint lit her eyes before she slipped on her sunglasses. "I'm okay with the wind in my hair."

She shouldn't care what Bran was doing or who he was doing it with. After all, she was leaving Crush Island and setting sail for Independence Cove.

She shouldn't care. But she did.

Sigh.

The woman who'd texted him wore a skintight dress that left little to the imagination. Her chest was unmistakably the subject of the photo, but Addi had caught sight of a cute, pert nose and full red lips. She still couldn't believe he'd canceled his date with that woman to ferry Addi to Lake Tahoe.

A rock song played on satellite radio and he sang along, slightly out of tune. She smirked, liking his voice no matter how imperfect the pitch.

"Are you laughing at my singing?" he asked, the wind from the open windows whipping his hair around his head.

"Not at all," she lied.

"Yes, you were." He turned the volume down. "It's

okay. My sister's been laughing at me since she was born." They watched the road for a beat before he added, "I haven't been to Tahoe in about five years. Last time I was there, I nearly died on a bunny slope."

"You mean there's something you can't do?" She gasped.

"I can't do a lot of things. Ski, propose, land CEO." He said it with a self-deprecating smile and followed it with one of his signature knee-weakening winks. Maybe one day when he did that, her knees *wouldn't* weaken. #Goals.

"I've only been there once. Joe's family brought us. I don't like skiing—it's cold and hurts when you fall down. But he was an amazing skier." That trip with the Harts was eons ago and mentioning it made her miss Joe anew. This weekend promised to be full of old memories that were hard to think about.

"Who's Joe?" Bran glanced over. "Old boyfriend?"

"We were friends."

"Ah, so he had a thing for you and you shot him down."

"Nothing like that. Our families were friends." Emphasis on the *were*. Her parents blamed her for quitting her position at Hart Media and "driving a wedge" between them and their wealthiest friends. Emphasis on the *wealthy* part. She'd always wondered if her parents were enamored more with the Harts' financial status than them as people. They were billionaires, after all. Like the man sitting next to her.

"Nope. I don't buy it. A romantic ski trip together—"

"We were seventeen!" she argued with a laugh.

"Even worse! He was probably dying for you to notice him."

Bran didn't know that her friend had, in fact, died. But that reference wasn't what caused her eyes to mist over. It was remembering the good times she and Joe had together. That ski trip was one of the best weekends of her life. They'd grown apart after she'd stopped working for his parents. Years later they'd reconnected for a double date, but she felt the distance between them. She recalled vividly the sad smile he'd given her while his girlfriend at the time and Addi's frat-boy date were talking about a football game.

She blinked away fresh tears and turned to focus on the passing landscape out her window.

"Oh, hell. What happened?" Bran asked. "You okay?"

"I'm fine." She gave him a watery smile. "Joe and I drifted apart. It was…hard."

"Oh." Bran drew out the word with a sage nod. "You liked him and he didn't like you, right? I'm sorry, Ad. That sucks."

She had the sudden urge to laugh. Or punch him. Or maybe laugh and *then* punch him. Did he hear himself? She liked *him* and he didn't like her back and it did suck! "We were friends. And now…"

She shook her head, the lump in her throat cutting off the rest of her sentence. She cleared her throat and tried again. "This weekend is Joe's life celebration. He prearranged three nights in Tahoe for close family and friends before he died."

The only sounds in the car were the low volume of

the radio and the wind sliding off the sleek sports car as they glided down the highway.

"I'm so sorry, Addison. I didn't know."

"How could you have?"

"How'd he die?"

"Bone cancer. From diagnosis to the end, he only lived nine months. The same amount of time it took for him to come into the world was the same amount of time it took for him to leave."

He squeezed her hand. "That's why you were crying in the office."

Bran would be so easy to lean on, to confide in. To trust with her deepest, darkest fears and secrets. She slipped her hand from his to dig through her purse for a tissue and found herself doing just that.

"We grew apart after I went to college," she said as she dried her eyes. "It wasn't as hard as I thought it would be. Maybe we outgrew each other."

"Yeah. I know what you mean." His comment was thoughtful, and she wondered if he was referring to Taylor, who'd been a family friend for decades before Bran and she had dated.

Joe didn't have a girlfriend when he died. He'd never married. When Addi heard he was sick, her own life seemed shorter.

Which was why it was a good idea for her to get over Brannon. She could be dating someone who was madly in love with her, not torturing herself by hoping her boss might someday notice her.

She punched the volume button on the radio to drown out those thoughts.

"I love this song!" she called out.

"Yeah, me, too!" he called back, cranking the volume louder.

She didn't know if he was letting her off the hook or if he really did love this song, but she was going to embrace the opportunity to stop being so damn needy. So far, their road trip had consisted of awkward pauses, tears for Joe and jealousy over the woman that would have occupied Bran's bed tonight if Addi's car hadn't broken down.

She'd learned a long time ago that relying on others for her basic needs came with strings, rules and, if Addi didn't follow those rules to a T, rejection. She was grateful to Bran for a lot of reasons—her job, primarily, but also that he cared enough to console her and drive her to Lake Tahoe.

But.

Her heart was a terrible translator. Her heart would read that professional concern as "true love" and fill her pragmatic mind with head-in-the-clouds fluff.

She was done pretending they might someday march down a long, white aisle. It was time to buckle down and be practical. Find that independent version of herself and put *her* in charge of her life for a change.

Six

The last hour had passed easily. Addison was a good deejay, even though she was cranking a country station. Not typically what he preferred but he could tolerate Florida Georgia Line. Besides, she looked cute singing along to every word.

He hadn't gotten over the news that a funeral was her "family reunion."

She kept her personal life a hell of a lot closer to the chest than he'd previously thought. He knew she was a private person, but good God. How had she not trusted him enough to confide that a close friend of hers had passed away?

What he knew about Addi wouldn't fill a shot glass. For good reason. Work stayed at work and she was at work. Now with the rare opportunity of having her outside of work, he was finding out all sorts of things about her. Like that she didn't like skiing. That her family wasn't close. That her late friend Joe was the son of the Hart Media Harts—a behemoth that made ThomKnox look like a garage start-up company.

Meanwhile, she'd clammed up. She was a lot like the tide. Advance, withdraw. Advance. Withdraw. He still felt as if she was hiding something from him.

But what?

He thought back to his conversation with Taylor—when she confessed she was worried about him. He suspected Addi was doing the same. And as much as he appreciated it, he needed to let her know that he was just fine, thank you very much. There was no reason for her to take on his personal life—only his professional one.

As he caught sight of her mouth moving to the words of the song, again he felt attraction vibrate the air. It was so much stronger outside the office.

He rolled up the windows and, risking potentially embarrassing both of them, tapped the Off button for the radio on his steering wheel.

"You don't like that song?" she asked.

"We've been politely skirting a very big issue since Taylor insinuated that you and I should date."

Addi froze.

"In this space, I'm not your boss. You can say whatever you like to me and I'll respond honestly. The impact of what we say will never leave the confines of this car. Agreed?"

She said nothing, watching him cautiously.

"I never should have dated Taylor." It was the most

he'd said to Addi on the topic, but the air needed clearing. "She and I are friends, great friends. Hell, we never even slept together."

"Thank God," she breathed and he shot her a startled look. "For your brother's sake, I mean. And your niece's. Or nephew's. I'm sorry, go on."

"Uh, right. Point is, you don't have to worry about me. I wanted CEO but I also love what I do. And while I admit I find you very attractive and funny and smart, I also know you are irreplaceable, and I'd never compromise our most important union. The relationship we have at work."

More silence from her side of the car, but she did nod. Eyes on the road, he continued, content to fully bury this hatchet once and for all, "I have no plans to ask you on a date, Addison." He glanced over at her. "None. Dinner tonight will be a couple of coworkers hanging out, and that's it. If you're uncomfortable or if you feel I've overstepped, say the word. It's not worth ruining our friendship."

She didn't respond to that either, watching out the windshield, eyes unblinking.

Granted, this wasn't the easiest conversation to have. The promise never to ask her out was as much to reassure her as to remind himself that she wasn't going to grace his bedsheets. Before their joking was misconstrued as flirting, or his lingering gazes made things worse for both of them, he had to set them back on course.

"You've been at my side as my executive assistant for a year and just so you know, I see that as a lateral position. You're every bit as important as me to ThomKnox. If I lost you, Ad, I'd be lost. And unlike your friend Joe, I know in my gut—to the soles of my feet—that you don't like me that way. You don't have to worry about me assuming otherwise."

She'd started out shocked, slipped into nervous and advanced to royally pissed off during Brannon Knox's monologue. He'd made a ton of assumptions despite promising he wasn't. He wanted to be honest? Oh, *she* could be honest.

How many arguments had she had with her parents over the years where they claimed to know exactly what she wanted? Exactly what she *needed*? Piano lessons. Modeling sessions. Cheerleading practice. She'd kept her mouth shut then, too, not wanting to disappoint them. Afraid that if she disagreed, they'd cut her off.

Then one day they did.

She'd barely graduated college before her parents were shoving her into an admin position at Hart Media. In a short while, she'd been "promoted" to accounts manager and hated every second of it. She tried for a year and a half to make it work—always at the encouragement of her parents not to lose out on the huge opportunity of working at Hart Media. When she was finally brave enough to walk away she'd never felt freer.

Her parents had been furious.

They were so certain they knew what was best for her, but never bothered asking her what she thought. Just like Brannon was doing now. By the time he got to the part of his speech where he said *I know you don't like me* she couldn't hold her tongue any longer.

"I do like you, you idiot!"

The words bubbled from her throat like lava from an active volcano, spewing out way too much truth for the confines of a car. Static electricity charged the air between them as her heart rate ratcheted up. She'd *never* yelled at him before. She had no idea what to expect. Was he going to yell back at her? Pull over and tell her to find her own way to Lake Tahoe? *Fire her?*

She hoped not. She needed her job. Liked her job. Liked him.

With nowhere to hide and the object of her infatuation a mere six inches away from her, she folded her hands in her lap and waited for his retaliation.

He didn't respond the way she expected.

"Oh."

That was what he said. *Oh.*

"I'm sorry," she blurted. Lame.

"It's fine."

But he didn't look fine. His mouth was a firm line, his elbows straight, his hands on the wheel in the ten-and-two position. She'd either blown up their friendship or lost her job. Neither of which she could face right now.

She stabbed the radio button and loud music crowded in with the heavy air in the car.

Seven

They arrived at the inn exactly when his car's navigation system said they would. Addison remained stoically silent for the remainder of the trip, and Bran, who was still trying to decide what the hell to think about their conversation, had remained silent as well.

She liked him.

And she'd called him an idiot.

He swallowed another laugh. Truthfully, that'd been cracking him up on the inside since she'd said it. He'd never heard her speak to him with anything less than professionalism and respect.

Which meant something he'd said *really* bothered her.

It was damn interesting, if you asked him.

Here he'd been barely banking his attraction for her this entire trip only to learn that the street went two ways.

He'd made a decision not to pursue her, to go have sex with someone else and dismiss the idea of him and Addi in any relationship other than the one at the office, but now...

Hell.

Now.

Screw the justifications he'd been making. Work was important, but hadn't he also argued that play was just as important? Plus, he and Addi weren't at work right now, were they? He'd thought she'd been offended about Taylor's suggestion that they should date each other— that Addi didn't want anything to do with him. Now he knew that wasn't true and it opened up a whole host of ideas, none of them rated PG.

The real bitch of it was that Taylor had been right. Hell, *Royce* had been right. He'd been the one to tell Bran that a woman who liked him was right under his nose. Bran had blown off the comment, convinced that the hearts-in-their-eyes couple had sipped from Cupid's Kool-Aid cup.

He parked and shut off the engine, leaning forward to take in the building in front of him. The inn was swanky and posh, smaller than he'd expected and fairly secluded. Surprising, considering the tourist-rich town. On the lake below Jet Skis and boats zipped along its surface.

He retrieved his bag from the trunk and, after a back and forth of "you don't have to" and "I got it," also won the right to carry in Addison's bag as well.

They were adults. They could navigate attraction. Especially away from work. Here, Royce and Taylor and Gia, or even his father Jack who popped in on occasion, weren't lurking around every corner. Here, they were just Addi and Bran. Which was new...and exciting.

At the front desk, Addison gave her name. The woman behind the counter consulted her computer.

"Lucky you!" the woman exclaimed. "We have a king-size room available. You two won't have to share a double."

The laugh that'd been trapped in his chest nearly escaped. This poor lady and her horrid timing...

"No, no," Addi told her. "We're not sharing. He's my boss."

"Yowch," he said in response. Addi ignored him.

"My apologies for the assumption." The woman— Ava, her nametag read—tapped her computer. "In that case, I'll put one of you in the king room and one of you in the double. They're the last two rooms we have available for occupancy, and side by side. So you're still lucky."

She took this mix-up a lot better than his coworker, who appeared, at best, mortified.

Ava smiled at him. "Are you with the Joseph Hart group as well, sir?"

"Sort of."

Ava flicked her gaze from him to Addi and back again.

"Uh, thanks for the ride." Addi grabbed the handle of her suitcase and her key card. "I'll settle in."

She fled the scene and he watched her, half bemused, half confused.

"Will you be staying the entire weekend, Mr. Knox?"

He'd planned on staying the night and driving back tomorrow morning, but that was before Addi admitted she "liked him." Not to be an eighth grader about it, but that seemed significant. Especially since she hadn't looked him in the eye since.

What the hell? He'd committed to playing harder, hadn't he?

"Yes, the entire weekend."

That overthinking part of his brain could stay dormant for all he cared. There was another side to him that hadn't been around nearly enough lately. The fun guy. The laid-back guy. That guy would have leaped at a spur-of-the-moment weekend in Tahoe. And with a woman who was as attracted to him as he was to her.

Ava slid a sheet of paper across the counter. "Here is the itinerary for Joseph Hart's life celebration. In case you and your employee cross paths this weekend." There was pure mischief in her smile.

"Thank you." He looked over the schedule. Cocktail hours, dinners, water activities and a masquerade ball. Weirdest funeral he'd ever heard of. "Looks like I'll need to pick up an outfit or two while I'm here. Can you point me toward the best shops in town?"

"Certainly, Mr. Knox."

He finished checking in and strolled to his car, his bag in hand. He had no idea how Addi would react to hearing he wasn't going anywhere. Guess he'd find out tonight.

She'd agreed to dinner regardless of what had happened during their car ride from River Grove, and he was holding her to it.

"You're the one who said you *liked me*," he said aloud as he turned over the engine. "No denying it now."

Whistling, he pulled away from the inn and toward the shopping area the clerk had told him about. Tonight was proving a lot more fun than his original plans, after all.

After Addison hung her dresses in the wardrobe and tucked the rest of her clothing into the dresser, she hopped into the shower. Just a quick rinse before she changed for dinner with Bran.

He was holding her to it—he'd texted her to confirm the time. She thought about canceling but canceling would be less mature than sprinting away from him like her hair was on fire. She couldn't hide forever.

But she could concoct a believable story.

Tonight, she would be courteous and professional... and apologize. She intended on remedying that rogue moment of stark honesty the only way she knew how.

By lying about it.

Blaming her outburst on grief would work, even if it wasn't fair to Joe. But grief was the only excuse she had. She couldn't erase what she'd said from Bran's memory, so she was forced to explain it.

This uncomfortable mess would be over in a few hours. One dinner with Bran and then he'd leave come morning. There would be a nice lengthy gap between today and Monday at the office. Which reminded her, she needed to book a rental car so she could drive herself home.

She swept her hair into a chignon and smoothed her

hands over her jade-green cocktail dress. She'd had no idea how to pack for a funeral disguised as a party. Her closet at home was choked with bright or pastel colors, but she'd packed her lone black dress just in case. She couldn't very well show up in fuchsia for the official goodbye. She'd die of humiliation.

Don't be dramatic, Ad, said Joe's voice in her head.

He was right. If she hadn't died admitting to her hot boss she liked him, humiliation wasn't going to be what took her out.

She'd just finished applying her lipstick when there was a knock. Heart hammering in her chest, she gripped the handle, took a deep breath and plastered a smile on her face. When she opened the door, there was no one standing outside of it. She leaned her head into the corridor and looked left then right. Empty.

The knock came again, this time from behind her. From the shared door between their rooms. Of course he'd do that. She resteeled her spine and replastered her smile before opening it.

Bran was, unsurprisingly, suited and sexy, his hair a tempting mess. His smile, unlike hers, wasn't manufactured. His stance mimicked hers, his hand resting on the handle of his own dividing door as if they were looking at each other from either side of a fun house mirror.

"You didn't have to give me the king bed," he said.

"You're bigger than me." Her eyes trickled over his shoulder to his room. The clothes he drove here wearing were folded neatly on top of the stark white bedding, his shoes side by side on the floor. His suitcase was open, still packed, which made sense. He was only staying one night. She took in each of the details as an observer, trying her damnedest not to imagine him sleeping, mostly naked, on that bed just a breath away from her room. She wondered if she'd hear him showering through the walls...

She silenced the thought since fantasizing about him while standing in front of him was poor form.

He shut his own door and strolled into her room, breaking that invisible fun house mirror glass to stand in her space.

"You're as organized as I imagined you would be," he said. "Clothes put away, suitcase tucked into the closet." Her heart fluttered when his eyes scanned her from head to toe. "Outside of work, I'm allowed to tell you you're beautiful in that dress, right?"

"Thank you," she managed. Barely. Outside of work and inside of her hotel room, there were a lot of things he could say and do that she could allow. Like a soft kiss to the corner of her mouth or a roll on the bed that would leave the comforter twisted into a knot.

Wait, no.

She had a plan and it didn't involve acting on her feelings for him. This weekend was about reclaiming her heart as much as her independence. He'd stated clearly that tonight was nothing more than two coworkers hanging out and she was going to honor his wishes. Just because she'd foolishly admitted she liked him didn't give her carte blanche to coerce him into her bed.

Suddenly hot, she stepped away from him—and the bed—to grab her purse. "We should get going."

"I booked a reservation on the balcony, if that's all right."

Sounded romantic, but then again when it came to him, even "good morning" sounded romantic to her. He offered his elbow and she placed her hand on his corded forearm and let him lead her from her room. Soon they'd be on the same page again and she could lull her feelings for him into a deep, forever sleep.

Eight

When Bran knocked on their attached room doors and picked Addi up for dinner, he didn't count on his body tightening at the sight of her standing in front of a bed. Seeing her, rosy cheeked and smiling up at him, had been the stuff of his recent fantasies—if she were wearing a lot less clothing.

Tonight, she wore a bright green dress the color of jungle leaves. The color made her eyes appear piercing turquoise rather than blue. Her pale blond hair was swept up, revealing her neck, and the dress had a demure square neckline that didn't show what she was hiding beneath. Unlike Tammie, Addison was a mystery. Not knowing only made him want to unwrap her more.

White wine poured, their appetizer arrived. Crab and cream cheese wrapped in cigar-shaped, deep-fried wonton wrappers served with sweet chili sauce. Bran wolfed down three of them before coming up for air.

"Damn, those are good."

"They really are." She blotted her mouth with her cloth napkin, having only made it through one.

"So, tell me—" he leaned back in his chair "—what's it like to eat somewhere other than Pestle & Pepper?"

Teasing her about her favorite restaurant in River Grove was low-hanging fruit. A takeout bag from P&P was sitting beside her desk at least three times a week. He'd needled her about it before.

"Have you *been* to Pestle & Pepper?" Her smile was confident, her voice strong. He liked this much better than her wide-eyed and dashing away from him.

"Never. Though considering how many times you come back with leftovers or carried-in lunch makes me wonder if I'm missing out."

Their dinners arrived—fish and vegetables for him and a chicken pasta dish for her. They each ate a bite before she spoke.

"You only know half of it. I eat there as many times for dinner as I do for lunch." Her nose wrinkled. "I'm not much of a cook."

"Me, neither. I love to grill."

They shared a not-uncomfortable beat of silence. Progress.

"What's so great about that place, anyway? Do they have some signature dish I should know about?"

"Their food is incredible. But the atmosphere, the people, are even better than the food. After college, I ate dinner with my parents a lot, but that changed." She was silent while she wound pasta on her fork. "I missed that feeling of home—a home-cooked meal. Pestle & Pepper is a close second."

It was the most he'd ever learned about Addi's personal life. In his efforts to treat his assistant with professionalism, he'd unintentionally kept their relationship on the surface. Shame.

"Family dinners weren't a regular occurrence in the Knox household. Dad worked a lot." Jack Knox was far from an absentee father, but it wasn't as if they were going to the zoo or the beach every weekend. Building ThomKnox had taken a lot of his dad's dedication and time. Bran thought of his own brief obsession with CEO. Temporary insanity was the only explanation. No way did he desire a schedule that demanding or pressure that intense. "Dad was right about naming Royce CEO. I was the wrong choice."

"Not wrong. Just…different."

"You must've thought I lost my mind this year." His eyebrows jumped as he considered her point of view for the first time.

She pressed her lips together like she had something to say but wasn't willing to share it yet. They'd get there.

"Consider yourself lucky you won't have the privilege of meeting my parents. They're arriving tomorrow afternoon." She lifted her wine glass and took a sip. "I assume you'll leave for River Grove early?"

Again, he sensed there was something she wasn't asking. Was she wondering if he'd be around for breakfast? Or attempting to ferret out his schedule in order to avoid him?

"Not sure yet," he answered. Now seemed the wrong time to drop the "I'll be here all weekend" announcement. "So, the staff at Pestle & Pepper treat you like family?"

"The owner, Mars, does." Her eyes warmed. "Last week he asked me to taste a new dessert they were adding to the menu. He took my advice on the cinnamon. Always more cinnamon." Her tempting lips curved into a smile of pride.

"I don't have that sort of treatment anywhere. Don't they know who I am?"

"It's not about status." She took the joke the way it was intended and consoled him by patting his hand. "I have a delicate palate."

He imagined kissing her and having a taste of her delicate palate. As he held her gaze, the air snapped with a now familiar electric current. Then she broke eye contact and steered them onto bumpier terrain.

"I need to apologize for what I said in the car. Again." She put her fork down and put her hands in her lap. "First off, you're not an idiot."

"Why, thank you."

"A-and I meant it when I said I like you—" her cheeks stained pink "—but I hope you didn't take it the wrong way."

He wasn't letting her off the hook that easily. "Which way would that be?"

"I like you. You're a good boss. A good work friend."

He felt his mouth screw to one side. *Work friend* made him sound like a balding, potbellied old dude.

"I think of you the same way you think of me," she added.

Naked, sweaty and in his bed? Because that's how he thought of her.

"Look at us." She gestured at their shared table. "Just a couple of coworkers hanging out at dinner."

That was verbatim what he'd said to her in the car. Satisfied with her speech, she smiled. She'd been so matter-of-fact while giving them the out they needed. She was hitting the undo button on accidentally admitting her feelings for him.

He could let her off the hook. He *should*.

But he wanted to live in the now, not the future. He wanted to work hard but play harder. Since learning the attraction to Addi was mutual, he couldn't care less about steering himself to a safe and sandy shore. Bring on the rocks.

"My emotions were unstable. Probably due to my grief over Joe," she continued, acting as her own defense counsel. "I was tired. Frustrated about my car. Worried about you leaving the office to drive me here. I didn't really know what I was saying."

The lady doth protest too much, methinks...

"I'm sorry. That's what I'm trying to say." She let out a soft laugh. "My reaction was completely out of context—I'm not sure why I said it."

He returned her smile and she eased back into her chair. She'd said her part. She'd made her peace. All he had to do was accept her apology and return to his dinner. Instead, he looked into her gorgeous cerulean eyes and said what he was really thinking.

"Bullshit."

Addi stared at Bran, fairly certain she was about to have an out-of-body experience. If she could consciously detach from her body and float away from this table, she'd do it.

She felt as trapped as she had in the car this afternoon, but now he didn't have to take his eyes off her to drive. Shouldn't he be relieved to hear she hadn't meant it? He was supposed to grab onto her explanation like a lifesaver and then float away, comfortable in the knowledge that his executive assistant expected nothing from him.

He wasn't doing that.

He ate a bite of his dinner like nothing had happened. She watched him chew, swallow and go in for more. Completely unfazed.

"I'm staying the weekend," he announced. *Fork, chew, swallow.* "Looks like I'll meet your parents after all."

Her vision doubled and she blinked at her wine. She'd drunk half a glass, so she couldn't blame that.

"I had to find a costume for the ball on Saturday, but this town is equipped for strange requests. I also bought swim trunks." He continued eating, listing various items on the itinerary as casually as if he'd been invited. "I'll stand in as your date tomorrow at Joe's wake. I'd feel strange being there alone since I never knew him."

"What?" she finally said. "Why would you come to Joe's wake?"

"For you." He lifted his wineglass and took a drink and she stared at him some more. "I was going to take in the sights but hearing how upset you are about being here and how nervous you are to see your parents..."

He shrugged, a casual lift of one broad shoulder beneath his dark suit jacket. "A *work friend* wouldn't let you go alone."

"That's hardly your responsibility." She didn't exactly snap, but her tone was definitely clipped.

"Well, who knows why I do anything. You did say I was an idiot." He flashed her a smile.

Groaning, she dropped her forehead into her palm. "I apologized for that."

"And for saying you liked me, I heard. Thing is—" he pulled her hand away from her face "—I don't believe you were overcome with grief. I believe you were pissed off that I said I wanted nothing to do with you personally, physically. *Sexually.*"

He paired the word "sexually" with the arch of one eyebrow and she had the irrational urge to dive under the tablecloth.

"At the time, I was trying to reassure you since I overheard you and Taylor talking at work. You said I was 'nice' which is the equivalent of you finding me as attractive as the calamari over at that table."

"Nice isn't an insult." But she had lied when she said she wasn't interested in him romantically. "I don't think you're calamari."

He ignored her awkward compliment. "We're in neutral territory here, Ad. This isn't work. I'm not your boss. Not here."

She swallowed thickly, her nerves jangling… It'd be so easy to say yes.

"We have the weekend. Why not?"

She blinked at him, pretty sure she was having that out-of-body experience she'd wished for a moment ago.

We have the weekend.

His wasn't an offer to explore their friendship and beyond, it was an offer for sex. At least she was pretty sure it was. And wasn't that what she wanted? Sort of. She wanted him, yes—she'd just wanted…more than his man parts.

Still, how could she turn down the offer for *those*?

She was so confused. And overheated. She shouldn't consider what he was offering—what he was *sort of* offering—but her brain was too busy throwing a party to hear her over the noise. "We, uh, work together."

There. That was logical.

"We work together well."

"Wouldn't this…" God. She couldn't say it. "This weekend change that?"

"It wouldn't have to." He watched her with a steady gaze, fork in hand.

She shakily reached for her wineglass. Sleeping with Brannon Knox would change everything for her. But not for him. He was suggesting they sleep together out of convenience, but she wanted something deeper than convenience.

"I'm not the kind of woman who texts pictures of my cleavage," she said, setting her glass aside.

He frowned.

"You can't swap me for her like we're interchangeable."

"I know." His head jerked on his neck like she'd genuinely surprised him.

"You shouldn't go to Joe's wake. You weren't invited, and you being there will make things awkward." She stood abruptly, drawing attention from the surrounding tables on the balcony. "Thank you for dinner."

She dropped her napkin onto her plate, grabbed her clutch and weaved her way through the crowded restaurant. She didn't look back.

"Way to go, Addison," she mumbled to herself as she punched the button on the elevator. She'd wanted Bran more than anything, and then when he offered himself to her, she turned him down?

Sanctimonious, Joe's voice announced in the back of her head.

"Shut up," she whispered as the doors to the elevator opened. The older couple inside gasped. "Not you," she reassured them as she stepped inside.

She could swear she heard Joe laugh.

Nine

She didn't spot Bran the next morning when she ventured out of her hotel room for breakfast. Nor did she run into him at the pool in the afternoon. There was no sign of his shiny red sports car from her window, but then again she only had a partial view of the parking area.

Evidently he'd changed his mind about staying the weekend, which ushered in feelings of relief and regret simultaneously. She knew turning him down was the right thing to do, but her hormones didn't.

She'd lain awake last night and thought of how she could have handled their conversation better. She could have talked to him about it—logically. She could have discussed parameters. She could have politely said she wasn't interested and then finished her dinner. Instead she'd overreacted, stood and stormed out.

God, she might have lost her job…

Not that Bran would fire her for turning down a weekend tryst. He'd never technically mentioned sex. He'd told her he wasn't her boss here. Which meant whatever happened between them happened outside of her contract at work.

Yes, definitely she could have handled last night better.

She chose the understated knee-length black cocktail dress for the somber gathering tonight. Joe wouldn't like it, but then again, he wasn't here. *So there.*

She blinked back tears, wishing he was here. He'd know what to say to her about this mess with Bran. Hell, he'd said it last Christmas when she'd shared in passing that she had a crush on her hot boss.

Go get 'im, Addi. Life is short.

Remembering those words made her suspect that she really had screwed up last night.

The wake was held in the Violet Ballroom. After passing the Clover Room and the Poppy Room, she'd figured out the ballrooms were named for flowers and not for colors. The decor in the Violet Ballroom wasn't purple but an understated and masculine navy and gold. A wide chandelier cast warm lighting over patterned carpet and the well-dressed crowd, mostly in black attire, milled around with drinks in hand admiring the photographs dotted throughout.

Joe's handsome, smiling face, surrounded by a gilded frame, welcomed visitors at the front. A table with candles and memorabilia and more photos stood at the back.

She'd arrived a few minutes before they were scheduled to start and the room was already packed. Some people she recognized as Joe's friends or family, others she'd never met.

His parents emerged from a small group and spotted her. The last time she'd seen Elsa and Randy Hart Addi had been packing up her desk at Hart Media. Since then, her parents had shared that the Harts didn't think much of her leaving them in a lurch.

"Beautiful Addison." Elsa Hart extended her arms and pulled Addi into a brief hug. Addi embraced Joe's mother, taken aback by the affection. "It's been too long."

"Yes. Yes, it has."

"Addi, Addi. Oh, we've missed you." Randy kissed her lightly on the cheek.

"I'm so sorry about Joe. I was honored to be included on the guest list."

"As if there was any doubt. You meant the world to him." Elsa's smile was warm. "He had it all planned, paid for and arranged." She blinked away fresh tears.

Randy wrapped his arm around his wife's waist in support.

"Are your parents coming?" Elsa's voice went flat, clearly hinting there was some love lost between them.

"No. Not yet."

"Well, do send them our way. It's been too long since we've spoken. And help yourself to a cocktail," Elsa added, cheerier than before.

"I'm told the emcee will be making some sort of announcement soon." Randy grunted. "After all that boy put us through, he's springing a surprise emcee on us, too?" He winked to show he was joking, his own eyes misting over. They all missed Joe so much.

Addi moved to the back of the room and meandered along the table stacked with trophies, ribbons and report cards Joe's parents had displayed. She smiled back at another large photo of Joe. His cheeks were healthy and full instead of skeletal like they'd been when she'd seen him last. Next to the framed photo was a memory board filled with photos from his life.

She traced her fingertip over the photos of her and Joe—one of him kissing her cheek, eyes closed while she grinned at the camera. That was Joe's twenty-first birthday. And another from a few years later, of them dancing at his parents' wedding anniversary party. The photo showed a scene more intimate than she remembered. Addi's eyes were focused across the room, but Joe's gaze was unmistakably pinned to her.

She'd never seen this photo before, and now that she was older and wiser, she saw something there she'd never seen before. *Longing.*

Joe was looking at her the way she looked at Bran. She watched Bran with a similar want. Meanwhile Bran lived his life in ignorant bliss.

Heart thudding, she turned away from the photo to catch her breath. It couldn't be true…could it?

She replayed her conversations, emails and text messages with Joe over the years. She recalled the final time she'd seen him. She'd sat with him on the couch at his parents' home. He was weak, but refused to let her see him lying down in his hospital bed.

"Promise me something," he'd told her, taking her hand in his colder one.

"Anything."

He glanced at their intertwined fingers before locking gazes with her. "Live a beautiful life, Addison. Not an acceptable life. Not an okay life. A *beautiful* life. One where you have the desires of your heart and leave none of them behind—including that boss of yours you're in love with."

A sad smile crossed her lips.

"Go get 'im, Addi. Life is short."

She'd been more concerned about keeping her tears inside than she'd been about reading between the lines of his speech. Had he left his desires behind? Had he wanted her but never told her?

"Oh, Joe," she whispered to herself.

She lifted a glass of bubbly from a passing tray and took a fizzy gulp, remembering how she and Joe had laughed any time his parents or hers had insinuated they should be together. Joe hadn't taken them seriously. Or so she'd thought.

Tears balanced on the edges of her lashes, she started at a voice behind her. Joe's brother, Armie, stood next to Joe's framed photo, speaking into a microphone.

"Good evening, everyone." Tall, with thick, dark hair, Armie looked like his younger brother. He waved an envelope in the air. "The outside of this envelope literally reads, 'Do not open until my party or else I'll cut you out of the will.'"

The crowd laughed softly. Addi couldn't find her

laugh yet, even though she did send an eye roll to the heavens.

I saw that, Joe seemed to say. Funny, he'd been stone silent on the revelation she'd had a moment ago.

"I'm the mystery emcee, by the way. Another of Joe's surprises." Armie's eyebrows jumped. "Let's start, shall we?" He read from the paper in his hand, "To my beloved parents..."

Yes, Joe had plenty of surprises in store for this evening, she thought as she finished her glass of champagne.

Bran had already been to the Violet Ballroom. He'd introduced himself to Joe Hart's parents. When they'd asked how he knew Joe, he told them the truth. He didn't. He told them he was here in support of Addison, but hadn't seen her yet today.

He then visited the table of memorabilia and perused the photographs on a board. Addi was younger in the photos and still drop-dead gorgeous. There was litheness to her frame, as if her womanly curves had come later. She was polished and regal, like she was now, but her smile was brighter and wider in those photos than it had been lately.

In the one of her and Joe dancing at what appeared to be a formal event, Bran didn't miss the way Joe was looking at Addi. Like he wanted her to be *way more* than a friend.

Poor guy.

Bran had never longed for a woman he couldn't have—that he wouldn't allow himself to have—until recently. Addi had captured his attention. If not the same way as Joe's, damned close. She'd left last night asking him not to come tonight, but when he finished up his dinner and paid the check, he decided he wasn't going anywhere.

She was used to doing things by herself, but maybe she shouldn't be. And at a venue like this one, definitely she shouldn't be alone. Sometimes being strong meant leaning on someone you could trust.

He was a man she could trust.

Back at the entrance of the ballroom, he paused to let a couple walk in ahead of him.

The crowd was facing front, where a man on the stage read from a sheet of paper. "To my brother, Armie," he started, his voice wobbling. Joe's message to his brother was funny and heartfelt, and by the time the emcee sniffed and made a joke, it was obvious that *he* was Armie.

Bran sidled along the edge of the group before spotting Addi. She stood, hands gripping a forgotten champagne flute, her face twisted with sadness.

"The last message I have from Joe reads as follows," Armie said into the microphone, "Addi, you're the one woman I loved for as long as I can remember." Armie's eyebrows raised in surprise as he scanned the crowd. "We, um, we never made it down the aisle, but you have my undying devotion. Even though I'm dead. Go, beautiful girl, and grab ahold of that incredible life we talked about. Go get him, honey."

Addison's expression could only be described as shell-shocked. Every eye in the room swiveled to her.

She blinked a few times in quick succession, her fair skin turning an impressive shade of rose. Bran could practically see the question marks over Joe's parents' heads.

Bran wasn't surprised even a little.

She turned to slip from the crowd and he moved to intercept her, but an older couple blocked her escape before he could reach her.

"That's quite the announcement," came the man's stern tone.

"Hi, Daddy." Addi's shoulders curled in and Bran frowned. He'd never seen her withdrawn before.

The band in the corner started up the music again as the crowd dispersed and mingled. Bran hung back, close enough to overhear Addi and her parents, though she hadn't spotted him yet.

"Joe was in love with you? How could you walk away from him knowing that?" asked an older blonde woman.

"I didn't know, Mother." Addi's tone was less subservient, more impatient. "Joe and I were friends. I had no idea he felt that way about me."

"And who is this 'man' you're supposed to fetch?" Her father's bushy eyebrows were so low they obscured his eyes. "He'd better make a good living. God knows you don't."

"Is this mystery man the reason you quit working for Hart Media?" her mother squawked, hand to her chest. "Think of the life you could have had if you'd stayed! An amazing career. A marriage to Joe."

"And after all we did for you, placing you in that company. You could have been a millionaire by now! Never listens," her father grumbled to her mother.

Addi's chin began to tremble. Bran had seen enough. He walked up and slipped a hand around her waist. "Sorry I'm late."

Three sets of eyes were on him and he wasn't sure who looked more surprised—Addi or her parents.

"Hi, I'm—"

"Brannon Knox," Addi's mother breathed, stars in her eyes.

"Yes, actually."

"My boss," Addi interjected.

"And her date." Neither of her parents offered their hands, which was fine with him. He suddenly wanted nothing to do with them.

Addi's face flooded with alarm and gratitude simultaneously. She looked like she wanted to slap him and then hug him.

Or kiss me.

Sounded good to him.

"Missed you," he said and then he bent and pressed his lips to hers.

Ten

The entire building had burst into flames.

At least that was what it felt like the moment Addi finally, finally sampled Brannon's delicious mouth.

The kiss couldn't have lasted longer than a count of three. He hadn't ravished her while onlookers gasped. It was a simple kiss hello, but for her, there was nothing simple about it. For her, it was a slo-mo climax in a sweeping romance. Her senses were filled with the warmth of his mouth, the enticing scent of his soap and the low hum in his throat as he ended the kiss with a soft "mmm."

Hand on her back, he steadied her where she stood and she schooled her expression.

He pulled her flush against his body and having nowhere else to put her hand, she rested it over his taut abs. Just for a second, then she decided it was more appropriate to dangle her hand at her side. God. He smelled *amazing*.

"Glad to hear we have Joe's blessing," Bran said. "He was very special to her."

"The love of his life," her mother said. She smiled at Addi's suitor, appearing less disappointed that she'd failed to splice the Hart and Abrams family trees than before.

Addi's family didn't come from money, but they had it. They partnered with the right people, kept their wealthy alliances strong. Addi had heard so many behind-the-scenes conversations about how to "align" with wealthy people that she'd sworn never to use someone for her own financial gain.

Perhaps she'd course corrected too much.

Her job at Hart Media was fine, it was. But it was also not her calling. She wanted to work her way up, not be handed a position because of her status.

Her parents encouraged her to exploit their connections, to "get rich quick" rather than slow. Addi, frankly, didn't gave a damn if she was rich or not. She only wanted to be loved. Love in her family came at a steep price.

"ThomKnox is a very prestigious company," her father said to Bran, cheeks turned up into a plastic grin.

"Addi is exceptional, is she not?" her mother chirped.

"She is." Bran gave her a squeeze. She liked his arm around her way too much. "I don't know what I'd do without her."

"And now you're together," her mom cooed, "which I'm sure will mean advancement in the near future."

"Well…"

Before Bran wasted his time being polite, Addi spoke. This was one relationship she wouldn't allow her parents to exploit. "I'm executive assistant for the president of ThomKnox. That's pretty advanced."

"She's more than that." Bran squeezed her waist again, his eyes warm on her. Not only had he not gone home, he didn't seem the least bit upset over her leaving him to eat dinner alone.

Joe's parents approached, and she saw the perfect excuse to duck out.

"If you'll excuse us. Bran hasn't had a bite to eat all day. Shall we?" She widened her eyes at her "date," and he picked up where she left off, bailing her out beautifully.

"Another glass of champagne for you, as well. Nice to meet you, Mr. and Mrs. Abrams," Bran added politely.

Her mother called after them as they left, "Lena and Kerry, please!"

Addi steered Bran to an unoccupied corner of the room as the Harts descended. "At least my parents have to be civil when they're here."

"That was them being civil?" Bran asked, his eyes going to the foursome. Joe's mother embraced Addi's mother and Addi felt suddenly bamboozled. Maybe things hadn't been as tense as her mother suggested.

"My mom does enjoy making me feel guilty," she murmured to herself.

"They want what's best for you. Everyone's parents

do." He snagged a glass from a waiter's tray. "Champagne?"

"Thank you. For that. For everything. I've been… awful."

"You've been incredible." His smile was sincere.

Once they had a small plate of food each, she took her first full breath since she'd heard Joe's letter. She and Bran stood at a highboy cocktail table with a candle in the middle. Reminded of their dinner last night, she once again found herself in the position of apologizing. This time, though, she meant it.

"I could have communicated better last night," she told him. "Sorry for leaving on my high horse."

"It's okay. I finished your pasta. It was really good."

She smiled, giving him a headshake. He was too much. And too charming for his own good. "It was kind of you to show up here. I didn't know I needed saving, but here we are."

"No one should attend a friend's funeral alone. Though I'm questioning the 'friends' part after hearing his message to you." He watched her as he popped a sausage puff into his mouth.

"Aren't we both."

"What was with the part about you two never making it down the aisle?"

"I have no idea." She pinched the bridge of her nose. As if that would set the world right again. "Half of me wonders if this is an elaborate practical joke. If Joe is going to stroll through that door and yell 'gotcha!' He always was the life of the party." She realized what she said and offered a wan smile. "Ironically."

Bran's eyebrows rose. "A practical joke wherein he fakes his own death so that he can admit that he's in love with you at his own funeral?"

"Yeah. Probably not." She sipped her champagne, troubled by that observation as much as everything else that'd gone down so far during this trip. Her eyes tracked to her parents, still talking with the Harts. "I had to sneak away before I broke his mother's heart. I have no idea what to say to her."

"Don't say anything."

"Well, she can't go on believing that Joe and I were in love."

"Why not?"

"Because…" But Addi didn't know why not. If it was true on Joe's side, and made his family happy to believe he'd found love during his short stay on this planet, why not, indeed? "That's actually practical."

"That's no good. I'm fighting practicality these days."

"I noticed." That small kiss was the least practical act imaginable.

"I was practical to a fault earlier this year. I'm a man who can learn from my mistakes." He sucked in a deep breath. "I should apologize for the kiss."

Her lungs deflated. This was the real reason she didn't "go get 'im" as Joe had suggested. Bran had never shown any interest in her before, so why would one little kiss ignite a five-alarm fire in him now?

"You don't have to apologize," she said, hoping she hid her disappointment.

"That's not what I mean." His voice was low and

sultry. She faced him, the candlelight reflecting in his bourbon-colored eyes. They were nearly as warm as the flame itself. "I mean I *should* apologize, but I can't. I liked that kiss way too much."

She could only stare. "Y-you did?"

"Did you?"

Color him pleased when she didn't stammer or hesitate in her response.

"Yes," she stated clearly. "Yes, I did."

Now that was what he liked to hear.

Reaching across the table, he lightly touched her arm before taking her hand in his. "Have you thought further about my offer last night?"

Addi's bright blue eyes darkened enticingly. "I thought you'd gone home upset with me, so no, I hadn't."

"And now?" He lifted her hand and brushed her knuckles with his lips, kissing her once before lightly touching his tongue to her skin. Her lips parted but no sound came out at first.

"I—I'll have to think about it."

"Successful leaders make decisions quickly," he told her. He wanted another kiss like the way-too-brief one he'd stolen from her earlier. He wanted to give her time to respond. Let her explore and find her way. She seemed curious and he would be more than willing to let her explore that curiosity until both of them were panting for air.

"Brannon. We work together." Her eyebrows bent almost desperately, but the heat was alive in her eyes.

"Yeah, I heard. You're my executive assistant."

"Don't joke."

"I'm not joking." He was content to throw caution into the windstorm given their borderline combustible attraction. "Remember what I said. I'm not your boss this weekend. Just a guy who'd like to have a few more close encounters with you." He remembered her words to him at the restaurant last night. "And for the record, I don't think of you and Tammie as interchangeable."

"Of course. I knew that." She closed her eyes as if embarrassed by her behavior last night. He didn't like that look of shame when he saw it earlier with her parents and he sure as hell wouldn't stand for it now.

"I only asked Tammie out to take my mind off you," he admitted.

"Off me?"

"Yes. You've been taking up a lot of space up here lately. Too much." He tapped the side of his head. He could see she didn't know what to make of that. "Everything I've said and done lately is to make you feel more comfortable around me. In the process I began to see you differently than before. The easiest way to distract myself was…"

"With Tammie?" Addison finished for him.

"Guy math. One and one equals I'm an idiot."

At least she smiled.

"I'm so sorry to interrupt." Elsa Hart approached the table hand in hand with her husband. "I just spoke with your parents. Evidently this gentleman is Brannon Knox of ThomKnox. Which he did not disclose when we met earlier…"

The band of tension between Bran and Addi snapped.

Unfortunately, she threw him to the wolves, probably relieved not to have to address his offer head-on.

"One and the same," Addi answered. "I'm Brannon's executive assistant. I've worked at ThomKnox for a year."

With no polite way to extract himself from the conversation, Bran indulged Addi and Joe's parents. He came here for Addi, anyway, so had no other choice but give her what she needed.

And, if she decided to explore what could be between them physically, he'd give her that and more.

Eleven

Addison went to bed that night exhausted from… well, everything. Joe's gathering had taken a toll on her, alongside some extra unwanted attention after she'd been outed as the love of his life.

Bran was right in suggesting she didn't have to explain Joe's one-sided love for her to the Harts, though. They didn't ask about it in front of Bran, anyway, so there was no reason to bring it up.

It was healing to reacquaint herself with Elsa and Randy. She'd worried over the years that they'd hated her for leaving Hart Media and growing apart from Joe, but it turned out they didn't feel that way at all.

Once the Harts had interrupted her and Bran, Addi grabbed onto the distraction like a lifeline. Eventually they'd left the ballroom to retire to their individual rooms, and Bran hadn't brought up what Addi and he had talked about before.

Not that it mattered. His claim of "I'm not your boss this weekend. Just a guy who'd like to have a few more close encounters with you" kept her up, tossing and turning for quite a few hours.

Brunch the next morning was held in the second-floor lobby and since the inn was mostly filled with Joe's friends and family, it was impossible not to bump into someone she knew. So, she put on a happy face, poured herself a ginormous cup of coffee and went out to mingle.

Bran hadn't rapped on their connected doors this morning to wake her, but he'd beat her down here. He was in line for breakfast, chatting with a pretty redhead.

Addison watched them together—the way the woman tucked her hair behind her ear and batted her lashes. She was petite, wearing a pale green dress and sandals. Charm oozed naturally from Bran so Addi wasn't surprised to hear the other woman laugh, warm and inviting. All-too-familiar jealousy propped its hands on its hips with indignation.

She'd had enough of that emotion to last two lifetimes.

"There she is," he said when he noticed her standing off to the side. "Addi, darling. Come over here."

Addi, darling. Swoon.

He opened an arm and tucked her against him. She inhaled his clean, soapy scent. In the office, she'd hadn't had the privilege of being this close to notice.

He rubbed his palm on her bare arm. "I wanted to

let you sleep." The suggestive lilt paired with a kiss to her forehead sold the assumption they'd spent the night in the same bed.

The redhead introduced herself. "I'm Rebecca."

"Nice to meet you."

"He's told me so much about you. You two make a cute couple. Bran is very charming." To her testament, Rebecca didn't say that with an ounce of animosity. "Later we should hang out. Bran and my husband have a lot in common."

Ahh, she was married. That explained why she didn't mind hearing Bran was attached. *Fake* attached, but still.

"Allen's a tech guy, too. And I, like you," she said to Addi, "run the show at the office. We should have a drink tonight. Al has so many great stories about Joe."

"I'd like that."

Rebecca bid them adieu and took her full plate to a table occupied by her husband.

"Did you think I was flirting with her?" Bran asked.

"What? No!"

He raised an eyebrow but didn't call her on the lie. "Want some eggs?"

"Yes. Please."

Holding his plate and hers, he dished out a portion of eggs for each of them.

"You don't have to take care of me, you know."

"So you keep saying. Potatoes?"

"Please."

"I like a girl who likes her carbs." He dished out a spoonful each onto their plates. "You take care of me a lot, Ad. Remember, I'm not your boss this weekend. I'm your date."

"So you keep saying," she repeated.

All he did was grin.

"I appreciate your efforts with my mom last night," she said once he chose a table for them and placed her plate in front of her. He'd served her nearly as much as he'd served himself. She couldn't eat half of the food on the giant plate.

"What do you mean?" He ate a bite of potatoes.

"Talking to my parents isn't as easy as talking to yours. If we'd have stood there any longer, I'm sure my father would have asked a lot of questions about ThomKnox shareholders, company worth and other impolite matters."

Bran chuckled. "I'm used to it."

She scooped up a bite of her own breakfast. "At least Joe's parents didn't grill you."

"They couldn't care less about our shareholders. They have more money than God. Seriously, Thom-Knox doesn't have a tenth of what Hart Media has. Damn monopolies." He winked to let her know he was kidding.

"Don't you? Have more money than God?"

"We're up there."

And she wasn't. They were from two different worlds. Her crush on him had always been safe. Distant. It wasn't the stuff of real life. It was a fantasy, pure and simple. Only now the lines had blurred. It wasn't clear what was happening between them.

"Money aside, your family is amazing," she told him.

"I remember when I first started working there and I met you one at a time. Gia, Royce, you...and then your dad and eventually your mom. I decided that day I wanted to be a Knox when I grew up." She winced, realizing what she'd implied. "I didn't mean that in a creepy way."

"Sure you didn't." He kept eating, unfazed.

"My family's never been as generous with their love. It always had to be earned."

Who wanted to earn love? She drank from her coffee mug and raised her eyes when she felt Bran watching her.

"Hence the family dinners at Pestle & Pepper."

He didn't miss a thing.

"You don't have to earn love when you can pay for it," she followed that with a "ha ha," but he didn't laugh. In fact, he was watching her a little too intently. Like he was seeing clear down to her soul.

"Maybe we can stop by there on the way home," she said, happily changing the subject. "I'm having withdrawal. I mean...assuming you're driving me home."

"Of course I'm driving you home," he said, amused.

"I'll give you some gas money."

"Addison." He dropped his fork and swiped his mouth with his napkin. "Do you hear yourself? What kind of assholes have you been dating, anyway?"

"I don't date. *Because* they're assholes. Except for pretend funeral dates. Oddly enough, those turn out really well."

Earning another laugh was like being handed a million dollars. Who needed riches when she had Brannon Knox?

Four-plus more hours in the car with him to look forward to after an entire weekend spent in his company. She wouldn't know what to do with herself come Monday morning when he was in his office and she was stationed outside of it.

This weekend was originally meant to be the beginning of the end of her Bran obsession. Now Operation Get Over Him held another meaning entirely. Like getting *over* him. Or under him. She wasn't picky.

She smothered a laugh by coughing.

"The masquerade ball is tonight," he said.

"Oh, I don't expect you to attend that. It's a whole thing, with masks and formalwear." She waved a hand. It wasn't a big deal, so why was her heart pounding a nervous staccato, like she was about to be asked to prom? "If anyone asks where you are I'll say you were tired."

"And let you go by yourself? Forget it." He ate a bite of eggs and then added, "Who knows who will dance with you if I'm not there."

"I don't think people are looking for a date at a funeral."

"No, I guess not." He settled back in his chair and lifted his own mug of coffee. "Which brings us back to the discussion we didn't finish last night."

Dammit.

Silence settled between them. She didn't know what to say, especially since he hadn't yet asked her a question. But then he did.

"Have you thought about us?"

Only every day for the past year.

She sure as hell couldn't say *that*. While she watched him carefully, debating how to answer, a smile spread his mouth.

"Listen, Addi." He leaned forward, his voice lower and, if possible, more seductive. "You don't have to say yes. We can finish out the weekend as friends and, much as it pains me to offer, I won't kiss you again. If that's what you want, say the word."

His low voice swirled around her like a vortex, threatening to suck her in. She *really* wanted him to kiss her again.

"But—" he took her hand and held onto her fingers, his gaze unwavering on hers "—I really, really want to kiss you again. And again *and again*."

Oh, Lordy. Easy for him to say. He hadn't had his heartstrings tangled in knots over her for the last twelve months. He hadn't agonized over his own emotions because she was suddenly dating someone in the office.

She could either tell him no—but how, when he wanted her as much as she wanted him?—or she could consider this weekend a once-in-a-lifetime opportunity. An all-access pass to Brannon Knox.

Her earlier justification that sleeping with him was a bad idea had grown stale since the kiss. Since he'd approached her so openly and honestly. As long as she maintained some control in this situation, she could have what she wanted and escape unscathed.

"Okay, but I need to set a few ground rules."

He put an elbow on the table. "I'm not much of a rules guy anymore."

"We can call them guidelines." She nodded succinctly. She didn't want any bizarre vibes once they were back in the office. Setting parameters would help both of them know how to behave. "Tonight and that's it. Once the ball is over and we…do whatever we do, then that's the end."

"Okay." He nodded slowly. "I agree to your terms."

She smiled and he smiled back and there they sat at brunch, having made the craziest agreement of all time. She was buoyant, excited…and slightly nauseous.

One night with Brannon Knox. She was going to make it *count*.

"Should we shake on it?" She disentangled their hands and held out her palm, which he shook officially. Before he could pull away, she added the caveat, "I have a strict curfew of midnight."

"No worries, Cinderella." A barely banked heat darkened his eyes. "I promise to have you in bed before then."

Twelve

When she was preparing to come on this trip, Addi looked up "what to wear to a masquerade ball" on the internet. She'd never attended one, though she remembered Joe's parents having one at their house about seven or eight years ago. She hadn't been able to attend, but she'd seen photos online of Joe in his tux and mask, a pretty girl on his arm.

A costumed ball seemed so...impractical. At the time she'd been working her tail feathers off at corporate headquarters for a company that made athletic wear. Rhinestones and ball gowns weren't exactly part of her wardrobe.

Joe either had fond memories of the party, or he wanted his parents to experience another. Or maybe, like her, he found the idea of a ball preposterous and was having a laugh over forcing his friends to attend.

She'd done research before she chose her outfit, and learned that masquerade balls were formal and classy. Loathe as she was to admit it, shopping for a ball gown was fun—and bonus, she'd found one to rent. Logical, since this occasion was quite literally a once-in-a-lifetime event.

The elegant rhinestone-studded gown was sky blue and sparkled like a sea of diamonds wherever the light hit. It was formfitting and cut into a low V at the back, which was almost chilly in the cooler air of the lobby. The mask she'd purchased online. With its matching blue and silver gemstones, she hadn't been able to resist.

At the rental shop, she'd been floored not only by the elegance of the gown, but how she felt in it. Beautiful. Captivating. Shivers streaked down her arms as she spotted the Sunflower Room, where the event was being held. When she'd rented the dress, she had no one to captivate. Now she did.

Unfortunately, like the dress, she'd have to return Brannon after only one night. But oh, what a night it was going to be.

He insisted they find each other at the event. "A masquerade is cloaked in mystery, Ad," he'd told her. "Where's your sense of adventure?"

The ballroom's interior was strung with fairy lights, but otherwise filled with shadows. A band played quietly in the corner, soft jazz that added to the almost romantic, and definitely mysterious, ambiance. Many women wore dresses similar to Addi's, but in a rainbow of colors, bedecked in rhinestones and jewels. The men were in black, most donning formal tuxedos, though she spotted a few velour jackets.

She didn't know what Bran was wearing, so she scanned the crowd. Seeking him out in a group was nothing new—she always looked for him first—but knowing he was looking for her caused her stomach to knot.

She'd agreed to be his date for one night, and here they were, the masquerade ball a preview of what was to come. Her goal for the evening was simple, but not the least bit pure.

She wanted him.

Tonight, she was going to be adventurous when it came to Bran—it might be her only chance.

A woman in a slim black dress, her long, dark curls falling over her shoulders appeared in front of Addi.

"Choose your fate." Deep brown eyes blinked from behind a black mask as the woman offered up a basket of gold envelopes. "One of these cards is destined for you. Which will it be?"

Addi swallowed a laugh. Fate? In this basket? She highly doubted it. She chose her own fate. But, what the hell? Once-in-a-lifetime experiences should be savored. She held her hand over the basket and closed her eyes, wiggling her fingers over the envelopes before choosing her "fate."

"It's a good one. I can tell," the woman told her before leaving to offer an envelope to another guest.

Addi stepped off to the side of the room and tore open the envelope. Inside was a note in handwritten calligraphy that read:

Find someone wearing a gold mask and ask them to dance. Your future awaits.

Addi giggled as she dropped the envelope into her purse. It was like reading a fortune from one of those machines at the fair. "What is up with this, Joe?"

"You read my mind," came a female voice from over her shoulder. Addi turned to find a red-haired woman in a stunning red dress, a red mask obscuring her face. "Rebecca. From breakfast. What a beautiful gown."

"Right, hello. Sorry, I didn't recognize you."

"The point of this event. What did your card say?"

"To ask someone wearing a gold mask to dance. What about yours?"

"Mine says I have to buy a stranger a drink. And you're about to let me off the hook." Rebecca looped her arm in Addison's and walked with her to the bar. "We barely know each other. You count."

After they each had a glass of sparkling white wine in hand, Rebecca asked, "Did you come with Brannon?"

"I'm his date, but we decided to meet here."

"Ohh, young love. It's too sweet." Rebecca flashed a bright white smile behind painted red lips. "Allen probably won't last long. A wild night for us ends at eight thirty. Is Bran wearing a gold mask?"

"I don't know." Addi scanned the crowd for him again. "I haven't spotted him yet."

"To a night of intrigue." Rebecca clinked their glasses and excused herself, wishing Addi luck.

There were a lot of people here, but no sign of her parents. It was unlike them to skip an event this bougie.

She sidled by couples in clusters chatting. Some of the men hadn't bothered with masks, and she wondered if Bran had even worn one—let alone a gold one. The card commanded she ask someone to dance, and while she knew she could ignore it, she wanted to believe that fate had something special in store for her. Mystery and adventure seemed more in tune with Bran's world than hers, but in the spirit of Joe's final wishes, she would have faith.

Her eyes wandered over the crowd anew before she turned in the other direction and nearly plowed over a man in a black tux. Her eyes flitted from his bow tie to a face she'd seen in her dreams on multiple occasions.

Brannon Knox's staggeringly handsome face was obscured by a mask. A black one. She drank in the sight of him, from those whiskey-brown eyes behind the mask to his foppish hairstyle to his furrowed brow.

"Excuse me," he said, his smile measured and polite. Recognition lit his eyes a half second later. *"Addison."* His smooth voice sailed along her body like a caress. "You're—that's a dress. Sorry, I'm completely floored by how beautiful you are."

"A first," she joked.

"No, not even close. But tonight will be full of firsts."

Yes, she supposed it would. She pulled out her card and handed it to him. "You chose poorly." She gestured to her own mask. "Gold was the winning color."

He read the card before tearing it into pieces and tossing it over his shoulder. "Wrong again, Cinderella." From his pocket, he pulled his own card. It read:

A lady in blue is the one for you. Enjoy your evening together.

"I don't believe it," she said through a laugh.

"Well, I slipped the lady in black twenty bucks."

"No!"

He laughed, his throat bobbing above his bow tie. "I'm kidding. I drew it fair and square. Honest. Dance with me?"

"It's tempting fate, but how can I resist?"

He took her champagne glass and set it on a nearby table. "You can't. Which is my secret weapon."

The wink was a little cheesy, but not on Brannon. It only made her want him more.

On the dance floor, he pulled her close, his hand brushing her bare back. "This is some dress. I look forward to seeing you wear it into the office sometime."

"Sorry to disappoint you, but it's a rental."

"Bummer. You could've livened up the next staff meeting." He looked down at her, sincere. "I mean it, though. You are incredibly beautiful. In that dress or out of it."

She felt her mouth drop open.

"I didn't mean it that way." He hoisted an eyebrow so high it winged over his mask. "Or did I?"

"With you, who knows? Where has this funny, open guy been all year?" She'd meant it as a teasing statement but his chest lifted and dropped in a heavy sigh.

"I was different when you started working at Thom-Knox. More laid-back. More fun. Lighter, in general. Dad handing off CEO…" He shook his head. "I didn't want anything I was running after at the time. Isn't that something? I didn't realize it until later."

A great metaphor for tonight. He was running after Addi now, but in the future would he realize she was wrong for him? Would he look back and see how he'd behaved out of character this weekend, too? The possibility of losing her heart was a bigger risk than losing her job, and that was saying something. No matter how much fun she was having in fantasyland tonight, she had to keep her head on straight—for her heart's sake.

They swayed to the music—a mix of jazzy undertones and pop beats that was steady and smooth—like Bran's steps.

"You can't sing, but you can move," she said.

"Oh, honey, I can move."

She squeezed his biceps. "Not what I meant."

"And yet, our minds keep going there. Are you excited for tonight?"

"Very," she breathed.

"Good." He leaned close and spoke into her ear. "I have plans for you."

"I have plans for you, too." Emboldened by the mask, she'd said that aloud.

"Really."

She hummed, enjoying talking about what was to come.

"Care to share?" he asked.

She shook her head. "I'm more of a show than tell kind of girl."

Where did this brazen vixen come from? She smiled, liking the power she wielded. Especially when Bran tucked her so close the hard ridge along his zipper pressed into the front of her dress.

"How much longer do we have to stay?" he growled in her ear.

"A good, *long* while." She purred up at him. "I know it'll be *hard*, but I promise I'll make it worth your while." She erased the space between their bodies and he grunted when she brushed his erection. If what she felt against her was any indication of what it'd feel like without their clothes in the way, she was in for a great time tonight.

As if it could be bad.

Good point.

"Haven't we waited long enough?" Again, his voice was a husky growl. She'd never heard him talk like that, like he was balanced on the very edge of desire. She'd never seen—or felt—him turned on before. It was *wonderful*.

"I want you to want me a little longer before we go upstairs." She wanted him to long for her, to imagine her naked, to watch her, wondering how he could survive another second without her lips on his. After all, she'd felt that way about him for over a year.

"I didn't peg you for a masochist, Addison Abrams." He swept her in a smooth circle and she followed his lead. "I like it."

"Maybe, Brannon Knox," she said, swaying with him to the music, "you should have been paying closer attention."

Thirteen

Who is this masked woman?

Addi had danced with him for a few more songs. He liked holding her, being near her. The delicious anticipation of what would come later. *Her.* He'd guarantee it.

This weekend would forever be marked in her memory, and his. He was going to make it that good.

They found a seat in a dark corner. She sipped a glass of wine slowly while dropping double entendres. He flirted back, glad for the table blocking his lap—she turned him on more than anyone he could remember, and with just the hint of a smile. She was driving him crazy and he was more than ready to get the hell out of here.

By the time Rebecca and her husband, Allen, joined them at their table, Bran had been ready to *howl*.

If Addi wanted him to want her, goal achieved.

When she and Bran finally left the party, it had taken every ounce of restraint he possessed not to press her against the elevator wall and kiss her until they were both out of their minds.

He waved the keycard over the sensor on his door, looking forward to the feel of her hands on his body beneath this tux. To discovering what she was hiding beneath her dress. He wanted those full breasts in his face, in his mouth. He wanted to grip her ass and graze her neck with the edge of his teeth.

He wanted her with an animal need that was unfamiliar to him—had he ever wanted a woman this badly?

To keep from busting out of his tux like the Hulk, he reined in his libido as he popped open the door. She'd probably want a drink or conversation first. He wasn't going to maul her the second they stepped over the threshold. He was more man than beast…at least he thought so.

"After you."

She stepped in ahead of him. The room had been cleaned, the bed neatly made. He'd put his clothes away and tucked his suitcase aside earlier. Mentally, he mapped a path to where he stashed the condoms he'd picked up in town that first day. Wishful thinking at the time.

She set her purse on the entertainment stand and turned to him. The mask still covered her face, her bright blue eyes even brighter behind it. He'd taken his off at the table while they were still at the party and hadn't bothered finding it again when she suggested they leave.

He liked that she'd left hers on, liked the mystery of her, the idea of unwrapping her—every part of her.

Now he reached for the ribbon tied at the back of her head. "May I?"

"You may." Those pink lips. He hadn't had a taste of her tonight and was looking forward to a kiss more than anything. Their first kiss had been in public. Neither of them had reacted the way they wanted at the time, but now they were alone. She could go *wild* if the spirit moved her.

He kept his eyes on hers as he slowly untied the satin and lifted the mask from her face. Revealing her rosy cheeks made him look forward to revealing other parts of her. He kissed the apples of each of those cheeks and murmured into her ear, "I'm kissing every pink part of you tonight, Addison."

She didn't laugh. She didn't speak. But she did touch him. Her hands on his chest, she slid her palms north and tugged his bow tie free. Behind his crisp shirt and jacket, his heart thundered. The anticipation of wanting her had been sheer torture.

She unbuttoned his shirt, her hands shaking over the first three buttons.

He palmed her cheek and thumbed her bottom lip. "Nervous?"

"Excited," she admitted with a grin.

"You can't do anything I won't like. I promise." He wanted her to enjoy herself. Hell, he wanted her to have the time of her fucking life tonight. No pun intended.

"I, um… I don't know where to start. It's like seeing everything I've ever liked all in one place."

Damn. That was flattering. He watched her, wondering how he'd overlooked her for so long. How had he seen her day in and day out and not acted on the attraction so obviously vibrating between them?

"Start where you left off," he told her, placing her hands on his buttons. Seemingly over her case of nerves, she made swift work opening the rest of his shirt and stripping it from his shoulders. Leaving his arms trapped in the sleeves, she smoothed her hands over his bare chest.

"Mmm. That's better." She leaned forward and closed her mouth over his pectoral before dragging her tongue to the other and giving his nipple a light bite.

He sucked air through his teeth but she only smiled up at him. God, what did she have planned for him? Half of him wanted it right now and the other half of him wanted her to take her time and torture him some more.

Greedily, she explored his chest with her mouth and hands and he lost himself in the sensation of being wanted. He was used to doing the pursuing. He normally initiated the touching, the kissing.

He liked this dynamic.

She yanked his shirt from his arms and pushed him toward the bed. He sat, watching as she tugged her skirt up to her thighs and pressed one knee into the bed, the other straddling him. Once she was astride him, he had no option but to look up. To her fancy updo, a few locks of hair that'd come undone curling around her face, to her blue eyes, bright and seeking. Her mouth was a bow, her tongue the arrow as it darted out to wet her lips.

"How are you doing down there?" she asked.

He was as hard as rebar and just as unyielding.

"Keep doing what you're doing." He tucked a stray curl behind her ear. "I'm here for it."

He was entranced. Completely under her power. And he didn't mind one damn bit.

Fingers on his belt, she slowly undid the leather, feeding it through his belt loops and throwing it on the floor. She stroked his erection over his zipper and unbelievably, he grew harder.

When she unzipped his pants, she gasped. If she'd wondered whether he was a boxers or briefs guy, that conundrum had been definitively answered.

"You don't…wear anything under your pants?"

"Not a thing." He grinned, loving the hunger in her eyes.

"Ever?"

"Never."

"Wow. The office will never be the same." When her smile hitched, it snagged him in the gut, pulling him forward like a fish on a line.

"Kiss me." If he didn't taste her soon, who knew what would happen.

She tenderly laid her lips on his, stroking into his mouth with her tongue. He closed his eyes and drank her in, lying back and pulling her with him. His hands found her bare back, where her dress dove into a deep V, and he caressed her agonizingly soft skin. Slowly, ever so slowly, he dragged the zipper down over her backside, pulling away from her mouth to say, "I've been waiting for this moment all night."

She sat up, a feisty twinkle in her eye when she said, "I've been waiting longer."

He sat up with her as she shrugged out of the dress. Beneath, she was naked, her breasts pert. Beautiful, with pale peach-colored nipples and tan lines that made his mouth water. He reached up and cradled those breasts, pleased when they barely filled his large hands. They were so delicate. So Addi. He swept his thumbs over her nipples. His eyes fastened to them as they pebbled in the cooler air of the room.

"Oh, that feels nice," she praised.

"That ain't nothin'." He set his tongue to one, the taste better than the feel. She raked her hands into his hair and encouraged him to make his way to the other. He was a man who was willing to serve.

He swirled his tongue around and around, sucking her deep. As her breaths quickened, her hips moved of their own volition. She rode his lap but fell short of where he wanted her—where he needed her. Palms splayed over her back, he moved to lay her down but she stopped him with both hands on his chest and shoved him down on the bed.

"Stay," she instructed.

He obeyed, watching, amused, as she climbed from the bed to shed the remainder of her sparkly ball gown and kick off her high-heeled shoes. Then she undressed him, which was something he didn't recall experiencing with a woman *ever*—he could say that with certainty. She tossed his shoes aside, peeled off his socks, dragged

"One Minute" Survey

You get **TWO books**
<u>and</u> TWO Mystery Gifts...

ABSOLUTELY FREE!

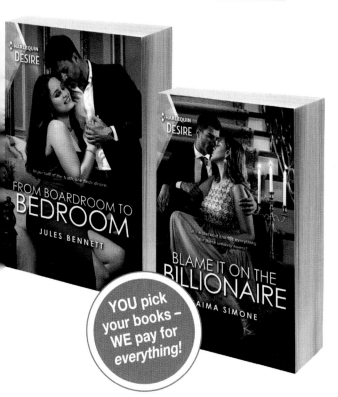

YOU pick your books – WE pay for everything!

See inside for details.

Dear Reader,

Your opinions are important to us. So if you'll participate in our fast and free "One Minute" Survey, **YOU** can pick two wonderful books that **WE** pay for!

As a leading publisher of women's fiction, we'd love to hear from you. That's why we promise to reward you for completing our survey.

IMPORTANT: Please complete the survey and return it. We'll send your Free Books and Free Mystery Gifts right away. **And we pay for shipping and handling too!**

Thank you again for participating in our "One Minute" Survey. It really takes just a minute (or less) to complete the survey… and your free books and gifts will be well worth it!

↖ We pay for
EVERYTH.

Sincerely,

Pam Powers

Pam Powers
for Reader Service

"One Minute" Survey

GET YOUR FREE BOOKS AND FREE GIFTS!

✓ Complete this Survey ✓ Return this survey

▶ DETACH AND MAIL CARD TODAY! ▶

1 Do you try to find time to read every day?

☐ YES ☐ NO

2 Do you prefer stories with happy endings?

☐ YES ☐ NO

3 Do you enjoy having books delivered to your home?

☐ YES ☐ NO

4 Do you share your favorite books with friends?

☐ YES ☐ NO

YES! I have completed the above "One Minute" Survey. Please send me my Two Free Books and Two Free Mystery Gifts (worth over $20 retail). I understand that I am under no obligation to buy anything, as explained on the back of this card.

225/326 HDL GNNS

FIRST NAME	LAST NAME

ADDRESS

APT.#	CITY

STATE/PROV.	ZIP/POSTAL CODE

© 2019 HARLEQUIN ENTERPRISES ULC
and ® are trademarks owned by Harlequin Enterprises ULC. Printed in the U.S.A.
HD-320-OM20

his pants down his legs and tossed them on the floor. Then she gave him another show, turning her back to him and tucking her thumbs into her panties. Bending, she peeked over her shoulder at him as she rolled the last bit of clothing over her temptingly round ass, past her thighs and finally off her feet.

His chest heaved, his fists mangling the neatly made bedspread. She came to him and leaned over, her small breasts brushing his chest as she crawled up his form.

Her lips barely touching his, she murmured, "Good boy."

Cupping her soft breasts, he accepted the kiss she offered, nearly exploding then and there when she kissed him long and deep. She took her time to explore his mouth while he gently pinched her nipples. When she gripped him and gave him a stroke he wondered if he'd die before he came.

"Bran." Her whisper was almost frantic. "I want you."

Best damn news he'd heard all day.

"I noticed." Sliding his hand between her legs, he found her warm and wet. He stroked her center, while he kissed her, timing his tongue with his fingers. But she wasn't able to hold her mouth over his whenever he touched that tiny, sensitive nerve bundle. She pulled away on a gasp.

"Condom," came her broken sentence. "Where?"

"Bag in the bathroom."

She moved to climb off him, but he stopped her with a "not yet."

"But—"

He reversed their positions, him over her, and with

one knee spread her legs wide. Then he found the heart of her with his fingers and renewed his efforts, kissing her nipples instead of her mouth this time. She squirmed beneath him, her hands fisting his hair, her breaths high and tight. By the time an orgasm rocked her, he moved from her breasts to kiss her neck, then her cheek and then her mouth.

"That's what I wanted," he told her, his lips against hers before finishing her off with a succinct kiss.

He watched her descend back to earth, shaking off the haze of the orgasm slowly. A smile crested her full mouth, her eyes barely open. "Thanks."

"My pleasure."

Somewhere she must've found a hidden source of energy. Next she pushed on his chest and rolled over him, kissing his neck and chest. Halfway to where he wanted her sweet mouth, she hopped off him and sent him a smile over her shoulder. Her hair was a wreck, and combined with the wiggle of her heart-shaped ass as she left the room, quite possibly the most tempting she'd ever looked.

Every moment he'd spent with Addi on this trip had taken him by surprise. It was a refreshing change from him trying to wrangle and orchestrate every detail of his life. With her he could just *be*.

When she returned, his head cleared of all thoughts save her. She straddled him, settling over his waist and waving the condom packet between them. "Ready, cowboy?"

He moved before she expected him to, pressing her back to the bed and snagging the condom at the same time. A laugh exploded from her chest, one of pure delight. He couldn't help grinning, too. "Are you ready?"

Her teeth on her bottom lip, her smile transformed into one that was at once demure and wanton. He knew why a second later, when he felt her hand grip him firmly before tickling his balls with her fingernails.

He'd fantasized about having her tonight, so sure he'd have to ease her into it. Take his time. He thought she'd be shy. That he'd need to coax her out of her shell by first kissing her from head to toe.

How wrong he'd been. Delightfully wrong...

He rolled on the condom, notched the head of his cock into her and her head bucked. Eyes closed, she hissed the word "yes" three times in a row. Her fingernails scraped his shoulders as he slid in the rest of the way, burying himself to the hilt in her tight heat.

Once there, he paused long enough to meet her open eyes, to admire the blush of her cheeks. "Ready, Addi?"

She gave him a squeeze with her inner muscles, grinning like a goddess while he nearly blacked out. In his ear, the silken caress of her voice announced, "I've *been* ready, handsome. Now start moving."

If he wasn't convinced before, now he knew for sure. Sex with Addison would be the best sex of his *life*.

Fourteen

Addi's goal for her one night with Brannon Knox was to take everything she wanted and leave nothing undone. She'd vowed to make it *good*. Evidently she overshot the mark, because sex with Bran wasn't good. It was freaking fantastic.

Epic.

Mind-blowing.

And when he'd stopped letting her run the show to take over, she was just as thrilled with the outcome.

But.

She still wanted to run the show.

"I want to be on top again," she told him as he stroked into her. *"Please."*

She could tell that he didn't want to say yes, to give up control of her pleasure. But there was more to her pleasure than he knew—most of it would come from being in charge of his.

Her *please* must have swayed him. He allowed her to climb on top of him, settling beneath her. Straddling him, she admired his hair ruffled in the pattern of her fingertips—*bucket list item!*—on the backdrop of a snow-white pillowcase.

She eased down onto him, and he filled her, the length and girth of him even more substantial in this position. Still, he didn't let her do all the work, his hands clutching her hips as he rose to meet her.

After a few gentle glides, he clutched her hips and slammed her down onto him.

"Oh!" What a lovely surprise that had been.

He repeated the motion, his gaze never leaving hers. Another orgasm crept along her spine, threatening bone-melting pleasure.

"Like that?" He pulled her down and hit that precious, perfect spot again.

"Oh!" He'd coaxed that reaction from her without trying.

"Yeah, you like that."

So proud of himself.

"You like this." She rotated her hips and watched as his smile was replaced by a look of pained pleasure. "Don't you?"

"Keep working, honey," was his gruff answer.

She kept working, he kept rising to meet her and his thumb brushed against her clitoris in time with each long, smooth stroke. It was that move that sent her over. Hands on his chest, she rode out her orgasm with her eyes shut.

Wave after wave hit her mercilessly, her insides clutching him greedily. He took over for her, pistoning his hips while she had the most delicious orgasm she'd ever experienced. A loud growl followed—his release—paired with his tight grip on her hips. So tight she wouldn't be surprised if his fingertips left imprints.

When she was finally able to open her eyes, she'd collapsed on top of him. Her breasts were smashed flat on his chest, her nose tucked into his throat. She took a long inhalation before biting his neck and soothing it with a kiss.

He spoke first.

"Damn, Addi. That was... That was..." His chest moved with a deep laugh and she used the reserves of her strength to lift her head. He quickly lost his smile and kissed her tenderly, moving his lips on hers.

"Incredible." He kissed her nose. "Unexpected. You're a cowgirl in the bedroom. Who knew?"

Delirious from her earth-shattering orgasm, she muttered, "Only with you."

"I'll take it." He dropped his head back and blew out a breath. "I owe you a few hours of foreplay, but if you give me a few minutes to recover..."

A few minutes.

Well, they'd have to hold her funeral right after Joe's because she must have died from ecstasy. No way was Brannon Knox asking her for a round two.

She looked into his dark eyes. "You're—are you serious?"

"Usually it wouldn't take me so long to recover." Ever so gently, he slid from her body and placed a kiss on the center of her lips. "Honey, you ruined me tonight." With a wink, he climbed off the bed and went to the bathroom.

That seemed fair. He'd ruined her a long time ago.

He strolled back into the room a minute later and she feasted on the sight of him. Wide shoulders trickled down to a broad, defined chest to chiseled abs. His penis hung heavy to one side. At half-mast, it was still impressive.

"Hey, I'm up here."

She rerouted her gaze to his face to find him grinning.

"Nah, I'm kidding. I like the way you look at me." He peeled back the blankets and invited her under them with him.

She went, cuddling into the crook of his arm. "This has been... You've been... I don't know what to say except for thank you."

He responded sincerely, his lips pressing against the top of her head. "I know this is a tough weekend for you. I'm glad I could make it better."

She rested her hand on his chest. "I'm glad you're here."

"It went fast. The weekend's almost over."

Right. Almost over.

Almost time to load up the car and drive back to River Grove where she would sit at her desk come Monday morning. Almost time to forget that Bran wore nothing under his suit pants—impossible. Almost time to pack her feelings for him into a deep, dark crevice and forget about them.

"But not yet." He was suddenly gone, her head falling to the pillow with a soft *whump*. His head ducked beneath the covers, his hands on her breasts while his mouth kissed her torso then lower, lower and…

"Oh God." She arched her neck and closed her eyes. Definitely she'd died and gone to heaven.

Heaven was the only way to describe Bran's mouth.

Brannon woke the next morning to an empty bed.

After a *very* late night with Addison, he'd pulled the room-darkening curtain so they could sleep in—which he'd had zero problems doing. He could have slept through a 10.0 earthquake. She'd thoroughly worn him out.

He climbed from bed, scrubbed his face with his hands and opened the drapes. "Ad?"

Sunlight filled the bedroom, highlighting the tangled white sheets. He squinted against the brightness, smiling at the pillows they'd knocked to the floor during their exploration of each other. Shuffling to the bathroom, he checked the dark room but she wasn't in there, either.

Well. That was a first.

He'd never *lost* his date from the previous night. Not that he'd had many one-night stands. And after how good last night was, they'd be crazy to only indulge in one night. He hadn't had enough of Addi.

Before they'd fallen asleep, he'd gone down on her and she'd climaxed several times. They'd had sex again, and he went slow so he could watch each satisfied microexpression cross her face. She'd fallen asleep snuggled against him, and dead arm be damned, he was content to let her lie there as long as she liked.

Now, she was a ghost? It made no sense.

The clock on the nightstand read a little after eight in the morning. He knocked lightly on their joined doors, assuming she'd fled to her own bed in the neighboring room.

No answer.

He knocked again. "Addi?"

When there was no answer, he tried the knob. Locked.

He knew damn well she'd enjoyed herself—several times. She hadn't faked her reaction to him any more than he'd been able to fake his reaction to her. She'd turned him inside out, surprised him and made him want more. So how was it that she wasn't around this morning for the more he was ready to give her?

He showered and dressed before venturing downstairs. Brunch was in full swing, and he saw some familiar faces from the weekend festivities. At the coffee bar, he spotted the face he'd been expecting on the pillow next to his this morning.

Approaching from behind, he leaned over Addi's shoulder and dropped his voice low. "Excuse me, have you seen the woman who was in my bed last night? She vanished without saying goodbye."

She spun around, her mouth pulled into a soft "O" of surprise. "Brannon. Hi. I was… I couldn't sleep."

"That's funny. I could barely wake up."

"I noticed. You snore." She poured cream into her coffee.

He started to argue, but she spoke before he could. "Would you like coffee?"

"Sure."

She poured him a mug, then added cream and the perfect amount of sugar. She knew how he took his coffee and he had no idea how she took hers. She'd been paying attention to him for the last year she'd been working for him and he'd been… Well, not ignoring her, but definitely not paying close *enough* attention.

She handed him the mug. "Here you go."

Before she vanished a second time, he gripped her arm. "Where are you going?"

"The pool?" A closer look at her white linen dress showed the shadow of a yellow bikini underneath.

"How about some breakfast?"

"I thought you might be in a hurry to leave for River Grove so I was going to grab a quick swim before we check out."

One of them was in a hurry today, but it sure as hell wasn't him.

"Now that you mention it, I could use a swim. *After* breakfast. Join me."

She turned and walked to a table, her spine straight and her shoulders pulled back. Proper. Elegant. She was icing him. No easy smiles or flirtatious side-eyes any more. Even her offer of coffee had been as generic as if they were back at the office already.

They'd barely lowered into their chairs when a waitress approached and took their breakfast order. There were limited choices on the menu, which made choosing easy.

"Pancakes sound good. I almost ordered that," Addi said conversationally after the waitress left. "Just let me know when you're ready to leave. I can be packed in a matter of minutes."

Again, so formal.

"What gives?" He knew when he was being dismissed. He didn't care for it.

"What do you mean?"

"You left my bed." And now that he'd said it aloud, he realized how much it pissed him off. Not because she owed him anything, but because he'd invited her there. She could have done him the courtesy of telling him she was leaving. Or hell, leaving a note. "I had to scour the grounds to find you and when I do, you treat me like we're in the middle of a business transaction. So again I ask, what gives?"

He sipped his coffee. It was perfect, which irked him for some reason.

"You knew what this was." Her voice was barely above a whisper. "One night and a clean break."

He felt his eyebrows jump. "I didn't realize there was such a defined line between Saturday night and Sunday morning."

"I said midnight—"

"We went well past midnight." Last time he'd checked the clock over Addi's naked, sated body, it was nearly 3:00 a.m.

"I was trying to be practical." Her cheeks stained pink as she studied her coffee.

"I'm not big on practical any longer. Remember?" *Practical* hadn't helped him land CEO. *Practical* had him asking out a woman he had no sexual chemistry with whatsoever. *Practical* had him purchasing an engagement ring for the same woman, one he didn't love. As far as he was concerned, practical was damn *impractical*.

He'd insisted enjoying the weekend with Addi for one reason: he wanted to. Granted, he hadn't expected to enjoy himself as much as he had or he never would have agreed to her one-night rule.

"I don't want it to end like this," he grumbled, frustrated. "Not over pancakes before a four-hour car ride home."

She watched him, silent.

"Have you had enough of me already?" Having asked that he realized she could answer the affirmative, which left him weirdly exposed.

"No." She sighed, and in her hesitation he sensed she was feeling equally vulnerable.

"Okay, good." Great, actually. "How do you feel about extending the weekend? Is there any reason for me to be in the office tomorrow? Any big meetings? Unmovable conference calls?"

"I—I'd have to double-check but I don't think so."

"Even if there is, we can cancel. There's nothing more important going on than this."

She offered a gentle smile, and his shoulders relaxed some. He didn't often crave approval, but hers meant a lot to him.

"Addison—what's your middle name?"

"Jane."

"Addison *Jane* Abrams—" he reached for her hand

on the table "—would you be willing to stay another night with me? The *entire* night. Through morning. No vanishing."

She nodded.

"I'm going to need to hear the word."

"Yes," she answered and pride flooded his chest. "As long as my boss doesn't care if I skip work on Monday, I'm willing to stay another night."

"I see no bosses here."

The waitress delivered their breakfasts and he was forced to have an annoying interaction to specify that *yes*, he was fine and *no*, he didn't need butter. When she finally left, his eyes tracked back to Addi, who hadn't so much as picked up her fork.

"I'll try to leave you with enough energy for work on Tuesday."

Elbow on the table, she propped her chin on her fist. "I make no such promises."

Damn.

He liked her like this. Bold and fun. Open and lively. So much better than the controlled, *practical* woman he'd bumped into this morning.

"The entire night," he reminded her as he cut into his pancakes. "I might save some of this syrup for later."

As he took a big bite, she laughed. He loved hearing it. He also made it a point to ask the waitress for some syrup to go when she returned to the table.

Fifteen

The surface of the pool sparkled in the sunshine. They were on the rooftop, overlooking the lake, trees and mountains. Plenty of boats were out today, their passengers sunbathing on decks or following behind on water skis.

"Rather be boating?" Bran asked from beside her. His tanned body was stretched out on a lounge chair, arm thrown over his head, sunglasses hiding his closed eyes, a pair of yellow swim trunks covering her favorite part of him. Although, to be fair she had a lot of favorite parts of him. Starting with his hair, followed closely by the sharp straight nose, contoured perfect mouth, the column of his throat leading down to his wide chest. Her eyes traveled down to the bumps of his abs, a perfect "innie" belly button and long strong legs. He even had nice feet.

"I can feel you staring at me." One of those eyes peeked open and he turned to face her. His white, shark-like grin was cunning and reminded her of every yummy thing they'd done last night. If there was anything that made her want to leave the pool or the precious sunshine, it was the promise of more Brannon Knox.

"I'm not staring," she lied. "I'm thinking and happened to zone out on you."

He pulled off his sunglasses and sat up. And no, she did not miss when his abs contracted with movement. "Thinking about what? The hours of foreplay thing? I meant that. Say the word. Our rooms are a short elevator's ride away."

She couldn't hide her smile, and his answering one told her he'd read her mind.

Early this morning, she'd woken and rolled to her side to admire him asleep next to her. She'd realized with a gut-wrenching certainty that keeping her heart out of the bedroom was more challenging than she'd previously imagined.

By leaving his bed and climbing into her own, she'd hoped to pull herself up from the emotional tailspin she saw coming. She worried if she'd stayed there awake next to him, she would've watched him sleep, counting his thick, numerous lashes, or tracing the outline of his amazing body under the sheet so that the night would forever torment her memory.

And she thought she needed to forget about him. Because last night wasn't supposed to happen—and sure as hell wasn't supposed to happen *again*.

Now she'd agreed to stay another night with him for

one reason and one reason only: she still wanted him. She'd had a hard time compartmentalizing. The memories of the time they spent together followed her from bed to breakfast. By the time he admitted he wanted her again she'd been powerless to resist.

"I was serious before," she started.

"About?"

"About stopping by Pestle & Pepper on the way back. Since you've never been there." It was likely her only chance to take him. P&P was technically in River Grove, but she reasoned that driving by the exit counted as part of this trip. "Would you like to stop?"

"Heck, yes." With that, he slid his sunglasses back onto his perfect nose and closed his eyes to soak up some more sun.

It must be nice to not worry about the future. Then again, he'd worried plenty earlier this year. She remembered him taut with frustration when Royce had been named CEO. Bran had come a long way. She understood why he didn't want to think any more. Why he wanted to indulge in the present.

The difference was, his indulgence was a fun sex-filled weekend. Hers risked her very heart and soul.

Drama queen, Joe's voice whispered in her ear.

Am not, she argued back, but he was sort of right. Indulging in Bran didn't mean she had to be emotionally crippled once she arrived home. She should give herself some credit.

That's better, Joe encouraged.

"Look who it is," a familiar voice said—a real one this time. She shielded her eyes as her mother approached, Addi's father behind her. "I thought we'd missed you."

"Nope, just grabbing some sun before we, uh, check out." No way was she telling her mom and dad about staying another night.

"We were on our way out, but we can stay for a drink. Brannon, darling, would you like a drink?" her mother sang.

"He's sleeping," Addi said at the same time Bran said, "Sure."

So agreeable.

"Let's move to the café, dear." Her mother lowered her voice but not low enough when she said, "Much as I like admiring his chest, he should dress before discussing business."

"I'll hand it to her," Bran told Addi as they strolled inside. "Your mom has some balls."

She groaned. Her mother had been an embarrassing disaster. She'd grilled him about everything but his banking information, and even then, Addi had half expected her to ask.

"I'm sorry. They're completely embarrassing."

"It's fine. I was the one who agreed to a drink. Nothing I couldn't handle." His hand in hers, he towed her in for a quick kiss. She was going to miss that when they arrived back home.

At the front desk, Bran stopped.

Ava, the same woman who'd checked them in, smiled in greeting. "Good morning, Mr. Knox. Ms. Abrams."

"Morning, Ava," he said. "I need to extend our res-

ervations one more night if you have the space. We're
not ready to check out yet."

"I'm happy to extend your reservations." Ava's smile
was smug, as if she'd known something they hadn't. As
if Bran and Addi had been wasting their time by not
sharing a room in the first place. "Are you extending
reservations for one room or for both?"

"One," they said at the same time and Bran sent Addi
an approving smile.

Ava tapped a key on her keyboard. "Which one?"

His eyes on Addi, enough heat in them to start to
start a forest fire, Bran answered, "Mine."

"Good choice." A few more key taps later, Ava
looked up. "I have you down for one more night in
the room with the king bed. Shall I send up a bottle of
champagne or strawberries this evening?"

Addi laughed.

Bran didn't. "Both. Thank you."

As they walked to the elevator, his hand went to her
back. "You're learning."

"What does that mean?" she asked as the doors
opened and they stepped inside.

"You let me treat you without any pushback. Pretty
soon, you'll have no problem letting me take care of
you." The doors shut and in one smooth move he had
her back pressed to the elevator wall. "How about I take
care of you now?"

"N-now?"

He reached for the big red emergency button and she
grabbed his outstretched hand in both of hers. "Brannon. *No.*"

He tsked at her. "So practical."

He shook off her hold, swiped her hair behind her ears and cradled her jaw. Then he lowered his lips to hers for a warm kiss. He smelled of coconut-scented sunscreen and really, really good sex. Or maybe she was projecting that part.

"You're mine tonight, Addison Abrams. What do you think of that?"

"I think you'd better start as soon as possible." She grabbed his ass. "What I have in mind for you is going to take a while."

Turned out they had to first move her luggage into Bran's room before they—*ahem*—indulged. After a few hours of indulgence followed by a much-needed nap, they emerged from their shared room in search of a late dinner. The strawberries and champagne were lovely, but not filling.

In the downstairs bar, they ran into two other couples. Rebecca and Allen and two men Addison had never met before who were newlyweds: Dave and Cameron. Rebecca had waved Addi and Bran over and asked them to join them at the bar.

Bottoming out her second glass of wine, Addison decided she didn't want this day to end. But Dave and Cameron had an early flight, and Rebecca had hidden more than one yawn behind her perfectly manicured fingernails.

"I can't keep up with you West Coasters." The cute redhead didn't bother hiding her yawn this time. "In my head, the time hasn't changed."

"Don't listen to her. She's always in bed by seven," Allen joked.

"Same here," Dave said. "Cam and I have gone to bed at eight o'clock every night while we've been here."

"Well, we're not twenty any longer," Cam said. "Hell, we're not thirty any longer."

This led to a discussion from both of them that Bran and Addi should "enjoy their youth."

"What about you, Ad? Are you tired from your exhausting day?" Bran asked, pure mischief in his smile.

"Actually I'd love another glass of wine." They had time for another round of epic sex or three, even if she stayed at the bar a little longer. Bran had nothing if not stamina.

"Allow us." Dave dropped a twenty-dollar bill on the bar top and kissed Addi on the forehead. "Enjoy."

"To Joe." Cameron polished off his whiskey sour, and Rebecca and her husband toasted their late friend and then finished their drinks as well.

Once everyone had cleared out, Addi let out a wistful sigh. After spending a few hours reminiscing about Joe and hearing how each of the couples met, she decided that practicality was overrated.

If she'd stuck with her plan to "Get Over Him" she never would have experienced the wonderful moments they'd had together this weekend. Some of the best of her life. Because she'd followed Bran over to the *light side*, her afternoon had been filled with surprises. Including an evening of swapping stories about Joe, which had been cathartic and so very needed.

In a way, Joe's death had brought her and Brannon together.

Bran ordered another round and when two full wine-glasses were delivered, they settled into a comfortable silence. Remembering the life Joe left unlived added weight to the room.

"You know, if Joe really did think of me as the love of his life, that's sad."

"Why? Did you want to fulfill his dream?" Bran asked.

"*No.*" She gave him a playful poke to the ribs. "The opposite. I would have had to let him down easy. I might've broken his heart. He was my friend. I never wanted more than that." Her own heart felt broken admitting that aloud.

"You did love him. As a friend. What if that was enough for him?"

"Hmm. Love's tricky."

"The trickiest," he agreed.

"My parents love me, but their love has always felt like an exchange. Like if I behaved and did what they asked, I could trade my good behavior for some of that love. I longed for the unconditional kind. The kind of love *your* family has so much of it's bursting at the seams."

"I've met your parents a few times now. They love you. I can tell they want what's best for you even if they have a harsh way of showing it. Their scheming is born of worry."

"I never thought of it that way." She'd only felt crit-icized or punished. "I guess I was too busy trying to hustle. Trying to make something of myself—trying to prove them wrong. Have you ever felt like you don't measure up?" She wanted to eat those words as soon as she'd said them. Of course he had. "You must've. With your dad. With Royce."

He held her hand, their elbows resting on the bar top between their drinks. "I know it's hard to believe because of my daunting physique, but I am only human."

She rolled her eyes, though she had to agree with the daunting part.

"Like you, I put a lot of pressure on myself," he said, serious now. "I felt like I needed to win. Royce didn't do anything wrong accepting CEO. Taylor didn't do anything wrong by falling in love with him. Listen, I can't argue with you about my family. They're incredible. Gia, Royce and I, we stick together. We have each other's backs. I've always felt loved and know that no matter how many times I screw up they'll *still* love me."

"You are now witnessing the jealousy of an only child." She pointed to herself but was only half kidding.

"My family adores you, too, you know. I've told them again and again how lucky I am to have you. You're a crucial part of ThomKnox. You want a family to appreciate you? You don't want to be alone anymore? *Addi.*" He kissed her knuckles. "You're not alone."

Hearing that healed some hidden part of her. A wound she didn't know was there. She'd admitted she wanted family, but had never truly accepted that she'd had one all along. "Thanks for saying that."

"I mean it." He kissed her knuckles again before

releasing her hand and then lifted his wine glass. "To family."

She raised her glass and clinked his, feeling very not alone for the first time in a long time. "To family."

Sixteen

Three and a half hours into a four-hour-long car ride and Addi was *still* buzzing from last night. Not only had Bran assured her she had a place in his family's heart, but he'd implied she had a place in his. And after he'd promised her she wasn't alone, he'd taken her to bed and made the most tender love to her. He'd been present and focused solely on her needs. She knew it was dangerous to project, but she could swear what he couldn't put into words he'd said with his body. She hadn't imagined their conversation afterward, as they lay snuggling and cozy in bed, talking.

"If I have kids, I'm having more than one," she'd told him. "I'd love to have a sibling or two."

"I always thought three was a good number," he'd said, tickling her forearm with his fingertips and sending chills down her body. "Royce and Gia and I have always been close. If one of us is acting like an idiot, at least there are two other honest opinions and no possibility of a tie."

She'd laughed at that, as she did at most of their conversation. Even though he hadn't outright admitted he wanted to have three children himself, that's what she heard. Her mind had offered up a vision of a small child on her hip, another's hand in hers, and a third one chasing Bran along the ocean's shoreline.

A fantasy, surely.

But what came next seemed to confirm it.

"I have a proposition for you," he said now, from the driver's seat.

"Sounds important. Let me prepare myself." She smoothed her hair—down since they'd left the windows up—and straightened her spine. "Okay, I'm ready."

"Honestly, when did you become such a smart-ass? I ruined you this weekend."

He so did, but not in the way he meant. He'd successfully thwarted her plan not to fall for him. She'd tried to keep her heart out of the bedroom but how could she when he'd been all heart?

"Which brings me to my question." One hand on the wheel, he spared her a quick glance before looking out the windshield again. "How would you feel about spending more nights together once we return home?"

Delighted. Thrilled. Sign me up!

"I'm having fun. You seem to be having fun." He lifted one shoulder in a shrug. "Why not?"

Not the profession of love she was hoping for, but

that wasn't going to happen—not so soon. She might've been in love with him for a year, but he'd recently been through the wringer. He was stoic about how Royce and Taylor and the role of CEO had affected him, she knew Bran—she knew he was still feeling his way forward.

She wanted to be more than his soft space to land. What they needed was more time to uncover what they could mean to each other. Exactly what he was offering. But. There was a real world to consider outside of this car.

"What about your family? What about work?"

"We can keep it to ourselves. Not because I'm worried about backlash, but who needs the pressure, you know? Who needs outside opinion on what we're doing when we know what works for us?"

Coming from anyone else, she might consider it a blow off, but this was Bran. She knew Bran. And she wanted Bran. So much she'd be willing to do almost anything he asked.

Almost.

"And this won't affect my working with you?" she asked.

"Not on my end. It might lead to a couple of very interesting private meetings—" his mouth quirked "—but I don't want you to worry that anything that happens between us will affect your job. I meant it when I said I needed you at ThomKnox, Ad. I do."

She needed him, too, but wouldn't dare mention it.

"I appreciate the transparency. I'm not ready to shut this down, either." She clucked her tongue and offered up a sarcastic, "Poor Tammie, though, what will you tell her?"

He chuckled. "You're never going to let me live that down, are you?"

"Probably not."

He reached for her hand and lifted it to his mouth. "A small price to pay."

A few minutes later, he swiftly pulled over several lanes of traffic and angled for an exit she knew well.

"Pestle & Pepper," he said in explanation.

"My home away from home."

"Let's have a celebratory lunch. I'm starving. Plus, they're going to wonder if you fell off the planet. Probably think their best customer was abducted."

She was still on the planet. But she was fairly certain her heart was orbiting Earth at the moment.

She was *so* screwed. Or was she?

Independence didn't have to mean being alone forever, did it? Couldn't she find a way to be at work with Bran and then be at home with Bran afterward?

Of course you can.

She wasn't about to miss out on being with the man she was already half in love with. She was going to carpe diem. He'd teased her about being too practical and arguably, he was right. Every fun thing she'd experienced this long weekend had been a result of her following her heart, not heeding the warnings offered up by her brain.

"Wait'll you have their lava cake," she told Bran as he pulled into the P&P parking lot. "You may have had lava cake before, but trust me, you haven't had Pestle & Pepper's lava cake."

"I trust you." He shut off the engine and climbed from the car. "With a lot of things bigger than lava cake."

She took his hand and they walked toward the entrance. Though she tried to stop it, her next thought was *like with your heart?*

She wasn't kidding about the lava cake.

It was damn good. The satisfying moment where the chocolate ganache oozed onto the plate was almost as good as watching Addi lick her spoon.

He'd had a hard time not thinking about her tongue elsewhere during the car ride back to his house.

"So this is my place," he told her from his front door. Before she could leave the foyer, he shut the door behind him and pressed her against it. "And this is you in my place."

She laughed, but he covered her mouth with his, tasting the chocolate on her tongue.

"But your luggage," she said as he kissed a trail down her neck.

"I don't need any clothes right now." He reached for the hem of her short dress and lifted it over her beautiful hips. "And neither do you."

He wasn't over how well this weekend had gone— and hell, it was Monday and they were *still* going.

He'd spent most of the car ride home thinking about Addi and work. He loathed the idea of boxing them in with more rules, or *guidelines* as she liked to call them, but Tuesday would come regardless. And he could admit they needed at least a loose plan.

He was as confident in her professionalism as he was in his own. No matter what the future held for him—or how far into the future they ventured—he was certain they could survive.

She unbuttoned his jeans and stuffed her hand inside, humming her approval. "Can I say again how much I like that you are not a fan of underwear?"

"I'm a big fan of underwear," he argued, his thumbs hooking the sides of her cute, lacy pink pair. "On you." Then he thought of what he'd said and quickly amended, "No, you're right. I don't like you wearing them, either."

He worked those panties down her legs and she lifted one foot, then the other to step out of them. While he had her here, he decided to have a taste of her, too.

Ten minutes later, one knee over his shoulder, Addi cried out, her shout echoing off the walls of his house. He liked her voice echoing off the walls of his house.

"I'm really glad we agreed not to stop," he told her as he kissed his way up her body. He tucked his tongue into the cups of her bra to tease each nipple while she gripped his hair.

"Where is your bedroom? Knees are weak," she mumbled.

He lifted her into his arms and started for the stairs. "I'll give you the full tour later."

"*Much* later."

"Much later," he agreed.

She held onto his neck, her blue eyes at half-mast, her smile his reward. A warning bell sounded in the depths of his mind but he ignored it. He was no longer the guy who was going to talk himself into a proposal or go running after a goal that had nothing to do with what he really wanted. He was smarter now, and he refused to plague himself with future plans and arrangements.

Addi was here with him now, and now was what mattered. Now was all that existed.

And *right now*, he was going to blow her mind in the bedroom and follow that with a long, lazy Monday off.

Seventeen

"Are you...whistling?" His sister, Gia, hovered in his office doorway, one eyebrow so high on her head she resembled a cartoon character.

"Can't I have a good day?"

Or a good week? A good *couple of weeks*?

He and Addison had fallen into a great rhythm since they'd returned to the office. They worked together, flirted with each other, and yesterday she'd come into his office and shared her Pestle & Pepper takeout.

She'd spent a few nights at his house when the evening went too late. No arguments from him. He liked her in his bed. Even if she was grouchy in the morning before coffee.

"You can have a good day—" Gia dropped a file

folder on his desk "—but when you smile like the Joker, it makes me suspicious."

Addi sailed by the doorway but evidently didn't notice Gia until she blurted, "Hey, handsome... Oh, uh, I meant to say Bran. Wow. So unprofessional. Hi, Gia. I didn't know you were here."

Nice recovery, Ad. No way was Gia going to let that go.

"Hi, Addi. How are *you*?" Gia folded her arms, her smirk evident.

"Fantastic." Addison straightened her shoulders and pasted on a smile that was a little Joker-y as well. "I was coming in to update Bran on his schedule."

"Do you mean 'handsome' here?" Gia jutted a thumb at her brother.

"Leave her alone." He stood and crossed the room, both females' eyes on him. He kissed Addi's forehead and faced his sister. "You caught us. We've been...dating. Try not to run and tell everyone within earshot so that we can have some peace, will you?"

"Well, well. Will office romances never die?" His sister's eyelids narrowed.

"You're one to talk."

"Jayson and I don't count."

"Uh-huh." He leaned forward to murmur into Addi's ear. "We'll talk later."

"Yes, um, sir. Bran. Thanks." Addi left the office, shutting the door behind her.

"You should be nicer," he told his sister.

"How in love with you is that girl?" Gia shook her head.

"She's not in love with me." He scoffed. "Who needs love?"

"Everyone on the planet?"

Ignoring that, he opted for a cavalier response. "Don't worry about me, sis. I get plenty of lovin'."

Gia groaned.

"Addi and I have compatibility. Companionship. We like spending time together."

Gia chuckled. "So you feel the same about her as you did Rusty."

"Best dog over." He gripped his chest. "I can't talk about him. It's too soon."

"You were *eleven*."

"Don't put a bunch of labels on Addi and me. It's not healthy. As far as you're concerned, we're just—"

"Dating?"

"Yeah."

What was wrong with that? No way was Addi *in love* with him. She wasn't clingy. Even the nights she stayed, she mentioned how she should be going home. He'd told her she was welcome to do whatever she liked, but if she chose to stay, that was fine with him. He'd grown accustomed to her rental car sitting in his driveway.

"It's working fine the way it is," he said. "We both know the deal. She's cool, by the way. You'd like her if you came out of your dwelling every so often to see what we do up here."

"I know what you do up here. My *dwelling* is only one floor down from this one, and tech is the command center of this entire operation." She spread her arms. "I see all."

"Now who sounds like a cartoon villain?" He didn't want to break Gia's heart and remind her that she couldn't have seen much if she'd only just now noticed he and Addi were seeing each other. They'd been discreet, but Gia was supposed to be the genius of the family. Though she was the first person to notice, so that counted for something.

"Mom's having a big cookout for the Fourth of July at the summer home."

"Already? I thought she was redoing the kitchen."

"She is, but she wants to 'encourage progress.'" Gia used air quotes around the words he'd heard his mother say multiple times. "She figures with a tighter deadline, the contractors will hustle harder."

Their parents' summer home was a huge estate in wine country perched on top of a hill overlooking a vineyard. It had been in the family since ThomKnox became a household name. It was also where Gia and Jayson spent their honeymoon. Which was, Bran guessed, the reason for her deep frown.

"Been a while since we've been up there," he said.

"Yeah." She sighed. "Jayson's invited."

"You're the one who made him family." Once a Knox, always a Knox. She'd been adamant about Jayson not being treated differently after the divorce.

"I know that." Her eyebrows crashed over her cute nose. "I just... How will I bring a date if he's everywhere I am?"

"Do you *have* a date?" His sister had been as single as a slice of Kraft cheese for as long as he could remember.

"I don't, but what if I did?"

"You would show up with your date. And then Jayson and Royce and I would talk behind your back about what a dope he was."

"Shut up!" That brought forth her smile. "I am perfectly capable of meeting a nice guy."

"I know you are." He wrapped his arm around her and gave her a squeeze. She was syrupy sweet underneath her Naugahyde exterior.

"Are you going to bring your adorable blond date?"

He slipped his arm from his sister's shoulders, dread settling on his back. Being at work and taking a little ribbing from Gia was one thing. At an *event* where they'd be clearly coupled off invited a lot of opinions and expectations. He didn't want to be under a microscope—not again. "I don't know…"

"You can't hide her forever." She pretended to zip her lips. "I won't say anything to Royce or Taylor—or Mom and Dad—but if you're really dating Addi, you can't exclude her from basic family gatherings."

She blew him a kiss and left his office, leaving him with a live grenade.

Addison at his family's cookout crossed a lot of boundaries he hadn't known were there. It opened them both up to everyone's assumptions. He wasn't eager to subject either of them to that. What they were doing was working. He saw no reason to complicate it.

This was, however, a great opportunity to tease her.

He popped open the door and affected his sternest expression. "Ms. Abrams. Come in here for a moment."

Addi smoothed her pink dress as she stood and walked to his office. With her blond hair swept up at the back of her neck, she looked like a dessert. One he wanted to taste. He folded his arms over his chest and leaned on the edge of his desk.

Worry crimped her forehead and he almost felt bad. He'd make it up to her soon enough. "Close the door."

She did as he asked, her hand resting on the door-knob like she was ready to make a swift escape. "I know what you're going to say. I'm so sorry. I had no idea your sister was in here. Obviously. I should have looked. That's no excuse. We're at work and I know better than—"

He crooked a finger, beckoning her forward. When she was within reach, he put both hands on her hips and pulled her to stand between his legs. "Kiss me like you mean it."

"Wha—"

Closer now, his lips brushed hers. He repeated, "Kiss me. Like you mean it."

She placed her soft lips on his and the brief worry he'd had about boundaries and who knew and who didn't dissipated. Addi went pliant beneath him, drap-ing her arms around his neck while her tongue danced with his.

She lowered to her heels, her eyes opening slowly. "So, you're not upset?"

"Have you met me? When am I upset?"

Why should he care what anyone said about who he was with? He was an adult. No one could tell him not to date Addison Abrams except for Addison Abrams.

He kissed her again and she pressed against him, breasts to thighs. This time when the kiss ended, he didn't loosen his hold on her.

"You *really* shouldn't encourage me." He was fighting a full-on erection at work. He was going to have to hide behind his desk until it went away, which at this rate might be tomorrow.

"And you shouldn't go to your next meeting wearing Think Pink lip gloss." She swiped his lips with her thumb.

"You are such a tigress. Had I known…"

"You'd have called me in here sooner?" She gave him a grin.

She wasn't wrong. If he'd known how much fun they could have together, he'd have called her in here a hell of a lot sooner.

An entire *year* sooner.

"It's been too long," Addi told her friend Carey as she sat down across from her at Pestle & Pepper. Typically, she met her best friend once a month for a girls' night, but this month had flown by. Must have been because Addi was so damned happy.

"It has! The last text I had from you was that your car blew up on the highway on your way to Lake Tahoe." Carey flipped her sleek, black hair over her shoulder, showing off envious cheekbones. They'd worked together a few jobs ago and had kept in touch. She was now an ad executive in Palo Alto.

They chatted about Carey's latest overseas trip, but Addi hadn't filled her in on any of the bigger changes in her life.

Carey glanced over her menu. "Is the car in the car graveyard yet?"

"Ugh. Yes. I have a rental while I shop." Despite Bran insisting she use a company car, she couldn't allow herself to do it. See? She was plenty independent! "It takes time to find a good used car. And I've been...busy."

"Aw, hon." Carey looked up from her menu. "Has work been hard?"

Addi swallowed her laughter. Their server dropped off their appetizer—fried avocado slices with jalapeño ranch dip.

"These are *evil*."

"Calories don't count on girls' night," Addi reminded her friend. They both dipped a wedge into the ranch before sipping their chardonnays. "Work's been great. I've been busy...elsewhere." She let the comment hang.

Her friend accurately gleaned there was more to that statement. *"Oh?"*

"I haven't had a chance to tell you... Well, I have but I didn't want to jinx it." Addi couldn't hide her smile. When she'd busted in to find Bran's sister in his office, she was sure he wasn't happy with her. Instead, he'd pulled her against his amazing body and commanded she kiss him. Uh, no problem there. Since then she'd on Cloud 999.

She'd been treading lightly since they'd been sleeping together, making sure not to crowd him. Making sure she didn't presume too much too soon. Bran showed no signs of slowing down. And before she left work today, he'd asked her if she had plans for the Fourth of July. Granted, not the most momentous of holidays, but it *was* a holiday. She'd told him she was free and he hadn't said more, only sent her a sly smile.

"There's this guy…" she started.

Carey's sharp, high-pitched cheer turned the heads of the patrons at three neighboring tables. "Oh my God, tell me everything! Is he hot, rich, great in bed?"

"Yes to all of the above. He's also my boss…"

But he was so much more than that. They'd spent many nights in bed talking after having amazing sex. They'd spent as many days ironing out work issues—working together as seamlessly as they always had.

She shared the highlights of her recent trip to Tahoe. From Bran driving her to staying next door to her hotel room to extending their trip one more night and then extending their affair.

"Is affair the right word?" Addi wrinkled her nose. "Sounds so scandalous."

"Agree. Let's call it a hot billionaire hookup," Carey said it so matter-of-factly that Addi burst out laughing.

It felt good to laugh. It felt good to be with Bran. Part of her worried she was in way over her head—with her heart dragging her further and further out—but for some reason that felt good, too.

As loathe as she was to admit it, she was enjoying living in the now.

Eighteen

Bran's calendar alert chimed on his phone and he tapped the screen without looking. Today had been hectic as hell, and the very last thing he wanted to do was walk to the other side of their floor and into a conference room to meet with Bernie Belfry, an old golfing buddy of his dad's who also happened to be a premium investor in ThomKnox.

Thank God Addi had arranged the necessary paperwork. He grabbed the bundle, neatly stapled in one corner, from the inbox on her desk.

His mood lightened some as his thoughts turned to Addi. It was hard to be upset about anything when they had a date tonight at her place. Sex made for a great release valve after work, which he'd always known. But sex with her was also completely hassle-free. That was a nice perk.

He passed Royce's office, intending to flip him off for sticking Bran with Bernie, but his brother didn't look up from his computer screen.

In the corridor, Bran came to the last conference room on the right and stopped, considering. They rarely used this one unless the others were full.

He was surprised to find the door shut, and even more surprised to find it locked. Before he could wonder what Bernie was doing in there, the lock disengaged and the handle turned easily under his grip.

"Catching a nap before the meeting?" Bran asked as he stepped in. He opened his mouth to continue the how's-the-weather and how's-the-wife small talk, but when he laid eyes on the person in the room, every thought shot out of his head.

Addi eased onto the conference table, her legs crossed. He took her in by snatches, his eyes moving too fast to focus. There were simply too many good parts to look at all at once.

Skirt: black and rucked to her thighs, revealing lacy garter straps attached to black thigh-high stockings.

Blouse: bright pink and unbuttoned halfway, revealing a wealth of cleavage.

Hair: down, tumbling over her shoulders in loose, light waves.

Hands: braced on the edge of the table.

High-heeled shoes: swinging in a rhythm that matched his own escalating heartbeats.

He shut the door behind him, grateful for the lock. Really grateful.

"Hello, Mr. Knox," she purred, her mouth spreading into a smile.

"Hello, Ms. Abrams." He held up the papers as he stalked toward her. "Guess I don't need this?"

She shook her head, pursing those tempting pink lips to say, "Nope."

He chucked the report into the wastebasket. A conference room romp hadn't occurred to him. Okay, okay, it had, but only in his fantasies. Being caught flirting was one thing, pants around his ankles in his place of work was another altogether.

But then that sounded too roped off and rules driven for his taste. He wanted to put as much distance as possible between him and the work-hard guy he'd been earlier this year. Taking Addi up on her offer of a boardroom tryst ought to help in that endeavor.

His eyes snapped from her chest to her legs. Damn. He had no idea where to start.

She solved that conundrum for him, grasping his hands and putting them on her breasts. Next, she snagged his neck and tugged his mouth down to hers for a scintillating kiss.

"How far?" she asked between kisses, running her fingers along the buttons of his shirt.

"What?" He blinked stupidly. "How far, what?"

"How far do you want this to go? My plan was to tempt you, but I respect that this is our place of work and if you—"

He smothered the rest of her words with his mouth

and unbuckled his pants, dropping them to his ankles as she laughed into his kiss.

"How much time do we have?" He didn't want to rush.

"Your three o'clock is with Royce and Taylor."

That gave him about thirty minutes before he met with his brother and soon-to-be sister-in-law. They'd forgive him if he was a few minutes late.

"You didn't give me long." He unbuttoned the rest of her shirt and opened her bra, freeing her beautiful breasts.

"I wasn't sure—" she gasped as he suckled her nipple "—how much you'd want to do in here."

"More than we have time for," he said on a growl. He tossed her shoes to the floor and lifted her skirt. The garters and stockings could stay right where they were. By the time he'd rolled her black panties down her legs, he was as hard as iron.

He slipped his fingers along her folds and found her wet and warm. Head dropped back, blond waves brushing the top of the conference table, she was a fantasy come to life. Behind her, a view of the mountains in the distance interrupted a perfect blue sky through the tinted windows, but the view before him was ten times as appealing.

"We need a condom, Addison. Did you prepare for that, too?"

She sat up on her elbows, her cheeks flushed. "Under the plant."

"Seriously?"

She nodded.

Sure enough, under the large potted plant in the corner was a square of foil. They were home free.

"You've done this before?" he asked, the condom scissored between two fingers.

"Yeah, right." She laughed, a glorious sight with her breasts bared in the air-conditioned room and framed by her bright pink shirt. "Who do you think I am?"

He rolled on the protection, shaking his head. "At the moment, I'm not sure."

Tugging her legs so that she met him at the edge of the table, he cupped her ass and held on tight. She wrapped her ankles around his back and gripped his shoulders as he slid in the first few inches. Her moan wasn't quiet.

Good thing those other two conference rooms were vacant.

He continued working them into a sweat, gently shushing her whenever her high-pitched cries threatened to be overheard. She covered her mouth with her hand, her smile evident beneath her palm. God, she was beautiful. And fun and incredible. He'd had no idea a vixen lurked beneath the polished veneer of his professional executive assistant. She was like having a naughty librarian on call.

Probably it was too much to hope for to gift her with an orgasm in the limited time they had, but it wouldn't keep him from trying. He navigated his thumb between their bodies as he entered her over and over again. By the time he lowered his tongue to her breast, he felt her tightening around him, her breathy sighs curling into his ear.

Her orgasm came not a second too soon. His release followed hers, though he was better than she was at monitoring the volume of his voice.

"Sorry. Loud," she panted before she kissed his ear. A shudder climbed his spine and zoomed down again.

"I hope I don't have to think in this meeting," he said. "Can't."

"Mmm. Worth it if you ask me." She kissed his cheek.

"Totally worth it." His hand on her jaw, he angled her mouth toward his when a sharp knock came at the door, followed by the jiggling of the handle.

"Helloooo? Is someone in there? We have a three o'clock for this room!"

Taylor.

Bran pegged Addi with a look. "You booked the same conference room?"

"The other rooms were booked for three o'clock!" she whispered. "I didn't, ah, think this would take that long?"

"You underestimate me." He gave her a hard kiss. "Don't let it happen again."

Taylor knocked and this time he responded. "Keep your skirt on, I'll be right there." Then to Addi, he said, "You should probably put yours on. Panties optional."

"What are you doing to me?" she asked with a smile as she scurried to redress.

He could ask her the same thing.

Addison's hands shook along with her legs. It was like she'd been submerged into a Jell-O mold.

Not only had Bran turned her on in minutes flat, but

he'd done it at work. She'd been excited all day, planning her sexy surprise in the conference room. The hidden condom was wishful thinking. She hadn't counted on actual sex, which explained why she hadn't considered the piggybacked meetings.

What was with her lately? She'd gone from consummate professional to hair-blowing-in-the-wind free spirit.

But she knew what she was doing. She was testing him. How far would he let her go? How far did he *want* to go? He hadn't said no to anything she'd offered yet.

That kind of power was heady. A rush that made her feel, well, feel a lot like she felt right now, only with a teensy bit of nausea at the idea that Taylor might've overheard. Addi had *not* been quiet while having sex with Brannon.

"Ready?" He wore a cocksure smile, his hand at the ready on the door handle. So proud of himself, and who could blame him? He'd taken her to the edge in record time.

"Ready," Addi said, not sure she was. He unlocked the door as she pulled his discarded papers from the wastebasket.

"I heard some…thing…" Taylor's gaze jerked from Addi to Bran. The other woman's darker blond locks were pulled into a neat ponytail at the back of her head, her navy blue dress outlining her baby bump. She looked gorgeous and professional…and suspicious. Her eyes narrowed. "Hi, Bran. Hey, Addi."

"Hi, Taylor," Bran said, sounding much more at ease than Addi felt.

Taylor's expression was blatant approval. "Well, don't you both look amazing."

Addi bit her tongue so she wouldn't laugh. She *felt* amazing.

"Thanks. I've been working out." He smoothed his tie, which was tied *not at all* right. The bottom was a good inch or two too high. Addi ducked her head to hide a giggle, then noticed she'd buttoned her shirt wrong. "Crap!"

"I knew it. You've been too happy," Taylor said to Bran.

"First Gia, now you? What's wrong with me being happy?"

"Nothing. At all," Taylor said sincerely. "I'm happy for you. And also—" she gave him a pointed look "—I was right."

"You better not have interrupted to gloat," Bran warned as he retied his tie.

"I came in here to have a meeting. Remember?" She waggled her ThomKnox tablet. "Addi, can you join us? Bran could use a second brain. His seems to be disconnected from his vertebrae at the moment."

Bran's eyes hit Addi and warmed an incremental amount. "Stay."

Her cheeks infused with heat and she couldn't prevent her smile. The request wasn't dissimilar to what he'd said to her on a handful of nights at his place. He'd wanted her to stay then, too. And him admitting it in front of Taylor was even more significant.

Royce appeared in the doorway next, tall, regal and frowning. His usual. Bran's tie was back to normal and the buttons on Addi's blouse were even, thank God. "Everything all right in here?"

"Why wouldn't everything be all right?" Taylor asked as she settled into a chair at the head of the table.

"I don't know. Seems…strange in here." Royce took a long look at Bran before his eyes landed on Addi.

"He's learning," Taylor said to Addi. "Men become more perceptive if you teach them. It's the repetition. Like training a puppy."

Addi snorted, while Royce and Bran argued against Taylor's assessment. Then they settled down for the meeting, Addi at the very spot where she and Bran had their own "meeting" a few minutes earlier.

While Taylor spoke, Addi thought about how she'd long dreamed of being a part of a big, loving family. And now here she was, one step closer to being folded in by the Knoxes. It was almost too much for her heart to handle.

Nineteen

By Friday morning, Bran couldn't figure out what the hell was wrong with him.

He should be in a phenomenal mood. The week had started with conference room sex, last night he'd fallen asleep next to Addi on her couch, and now they had the weekend to look forward to.

And next week was… *Fourth of July weekend.*

It suddenly dawned on him what was bothering him.

That warning bell that'd rang in Tahoe was back. He couldn't ignore it. The last time he'd ignored his gut had been when he and Taylor were dating. When he'd ordered a Tiffany & Co. diamond online.

Who ordered an engagement ring online?

A desperate guy, that's who.

There was no reason for him to freak out, which

might be *why* he was freaking out. Royce and Taylor and Gia knew that Addi and Bran were dating. They didn't care. Mom and Dad were retired. They sure as hell didn't care.

The only person who seemed to have an issue was *him*.

He hadn't officially invited Addi to his parents' house at the vineyard—and now he wondered if he shouldn't. She might not care if she went or not. Maybe a family gathering was too much too soon for both of them.

He blew out a breath of relief that brought his shoulders out from under his ears. He felt better now that he'd let himself off the hook. God, when was this day over?

He glanced at his wrist only to find, again, his watch missing. He'd left it at Addi's, he was sure of it, but every time he thought to ask her, he'd been in the middle of something else work-related. He was glad it was Friday—he needed a weekend like his next breath.

"Boxing tomorrow?" he asked Royce, poking his head into his older brother's office.

"No can do." Royce stood from his desk, his leather laptop bag in hand.

"Where the hell are you going? It's only—" Bran glanced at his wrist again before consulting the clock on the wall "—two o'clock."

"Home. I'm the CEO and I say none of us needs to stay another minute." He cocked his head, staring down Bran as if he could see through him. "Why are we boxing? Have some pent-up rage you'd like to take out on me?"

"Exercise this time, promise." Bran held up a hand and swore the truth. The last time he'd invited Royce out to his backyard boxing ring, they'd worked out some unfinished business. They'd both been feeling the pressure about who would be chosen CEO and their father had joked that they should box it out. There might also have been a come-to-Jesus talk from Bran that led to Royce breaking up with Taylor, but it all worked out in the end. Boxing had helped sort out the brotherly stuff between Royce and Bran, though.

"Everything okay?" Royce asked.

Not really, but that made no sense. "Of course. See you tomorrow."

"Yep. Have a good one."

Addi was at her desk when Bran entered their semi-private corner. He stopped in front of her, nearly forgetting what he was going to say. Blame the low-cut top. She'd never worn low-cut tops before, unless he hadn't noticed. He was certain he would have noticed.

"I left my watch at your apartment."

"Yes. I noticed." Her tender smile reminded him of that night. She'd found a new toothbrush in her hall closet and invited him to stay over. He hadn't planned on staying, but she was so damn sweet, he hadn't been able to say no.

Come to think of it, he hadn't slept much that night. He'd laid there for a long while, mind racing, eyes watching the ceiling. Addi staying at his place had never caused that reaction, so what made him itchy about staying at hers? His head was a jumble lately—maybe he was just stressed about work.

"I'm having the battery replaced and the face cleaned," she said. "You ruined your surprise. I'll pick it up after lunch."

The warning this time was a blare. Having his watch serviced and delivered as a surprise sounded like something she'd do for a boyfriend. Boyfriends led to marriage, which led to babies. See: Taylor and Royce. Then again, they weren't even dating when Taylor discovered she was pregnant and they weren't married yet.

Bran was suddenly overly warm.

"Thanks, uh, I appreciate it." He pasted on a smile. "I'll just… be in there."

He followed his pointing finger into his office where he drew the blinds and shut the door. Then he stared at his desk for a long while.

At the beginning of this year, he was sure he was going to be the CEO of ThomKnox, that Taylor Thompson would be his fiancée. That his life was on a fast track in a known direction.

Then it went off track.

His solution? Enter the unknown. Don't worry about consequences. Stop planning his life and live it instead.

"And now you're doing nothing but thinking of the future. No wonder you're losing it." He laughed to himself as he sat and opened his laptop. "Ad's right. You are an idiot."

And even though he mentally shook it off, he couldn't get past the idea that something had changed between him and Addi. Something she knew that he didn't.

Something that was going to threaten everything he'd just decided.

Forty-seven minutes later, Bran dropped the handset of his phone on the cradle and leaned back in his chair.

Scrubbing his face, he buried a yawn in his palms. A soft knock on his office door preceded Addison peeking through. He waved her in.

"That man could talk a caffeinated squirrel to sleep." He expected a laugh but all he received for his lame joke was the barest flinch of her lips. "You didn't have to wait for me."

"I—um." She handed him a black velvet bag. "I wanted to give you this. It's your watch."

He dumped the Rolex into his palm and examined the shining face. "Thank you. You didn't have to go to the trouble, but I appreciate it."

He unclasped the band and laid the watch on his wrist.

Addi sank to her knees in front of him, her eyes cautious, her smile shaky. "I wanted to ask you something."

"Whatever it is, the answer is yes." Especially if she was going to take off his pants and dive under his desk.

She let out a nervous laugh. "Oh, boy. You're not going to make this easy on me are you?"

He cupped her jaw. "I will *absolutely* make it easy for you." Get her a pillow, move to the conference room. Anything.

Her throat moved delicately as she swallowed but her ocean-blue eyes never left his. "Brannon."

That earlier premonition pricked its ears.

"Addison," he said carefully.

"You've meant a lot to me for a long time. A long, long time. I had no idea how much more to me you could mean. This…this has been a whirlwind and I wasn't expecting it. I know you weren't expecting it.

I know that right now, the last thing you're expecting is this."

Warning! Warning! Abort mission! Clear the area!
But there was nowhere for him to go.

Addison was on her knees giving him a speech. And with her earnest words bouncing around the room, there was only one way the speech would end. She wasn't offering a kinky in-office sex act, but something very, *very* different. Something he recognized, because he'd nearly attempted the same thing with Taylor, to his detriment, at the Valentine's Gala this year. A mistake he was saved from making by Taylor and Royce kissing at the gala.

Addi was about to make a similar mistake. He had to stop her before she said or did something she regretted— something she couldn't take back.

She flipped the watch over in his palm.

There, on the back of the face, was an engraving that hadn't been there before. An engraving she'd had carved into his seven-and-a-half-thousand-dollar watch. Two words, one question mark.

Marry me?

His heart hammered against his ribs like it was trying to escape. And because his mouth was dry and his tongue was welded to the roof of his mouth, he hadn't formed any words yet.

"I love you," she continued. "I'm totally and completely in love with you. I know you've had a rough year, but if I learned anything from attending Joe's celebration of life, it was that if I feel something I should say it. Before it's too late. You want to live in the moment, Brannon. So do I." She rested her hand over his and the watch and smiled. "This moment is real. It's happening. What we have is bigger than sleepovers and shared Pestle & Pepper. And by the way, can we go there for dinner because I'm *starving*?"

Her smile shook, but she glowed with happiness. With surety. She was waiting for his answer.

God. He was being proposed *to*.

He'd never seen this coming. That explained the tightening of his gut. The feeling that something was lurking just outside of his peripheral vision. He'd been wrong about her thinking of him as a boyfriend. She'd been thinking of him as a *husband*.

"You seem surprised," she said because he still hadn't thought of how to say no.

And he had to say no.

She'd gotten the wrong impression and that was his fault. He'd assumed they were operating with the same game plan, not that she'd gone rogue and created one of her own. The night he'd spent at her house flashed in his mind. Before she'd fallen asleep, she'd kissed him on the side of the mouth, her arm wrapped around his waist, and murmured "goodnight" followed by…

You're everything.

Which could mean literally *anything*…except not now. Not with a proposal engraved into the back of his watch. Now it could only mean one thing. He was everything to Addison, and while she was a lot of things to him, he simply couldn't be *everything* to anyone.

Trying to be *everything* had nearly cost him his relationship with his brother. Had left him with one hell of an identity crisis. Had taught him to take life a day at a time without scheduling every one of them in advance.

He'd taken a chance on Addi. He'd been so sure she was on his side. Not on the side of...

God.

Marriage?

He set the watch aside and grasped her hands to help her stand. He couldn't shoot her down while she was on her knees. He could barely do it now that she was standing, both her hands in his and raw hope in her expression. There wasn't any way avoiding it, so he'd have to say it. Say the truest, fairest words he could think of and then offer her an escape hatch.

"You weren't supposed to fall in love with me."

Confusion crinkled her forehead before a new emotion sent her expression careening in another direction. Fear. Sadness. Maybe a combo of the two.

"I'm so sorry, Addi. I thought we were cool with the way things were. Right now I'm not looking for—"

"Oh, no." She pulled her hands from his and rested them over her stomach.

"Listen, listen, it's okay." He rubbed his palms on her upper arms. "Here, sit in my chair."

"I can't sit. I have to leave."

"You don't have to leave, Ad." He wasn't sure how to fix this. But he had to. He needed her—here at work. And he liked her a whole hell of a lot after work, too. There was no reason to blow up everything they had just because she'd jumped the gun. "We can still go to

P&P for dinner. Nothing has to change. This was a misstep, that's all." He pointed to the watch. "I'm sure they can remove the engraving."

"A misstep," she repeated, not sounding convinced.

"One I'm familiar with. I know how you feel—"

"You have no idea how I feel. Did you hear anything I said to you?"

"I heard every word." She loved him. It was a gift. But the other thing… The proposal… "But, Addi, I can't marry anyone right now."

"Say what you mean, Bran. You can't marry *me*."

He didn't know if he'd *never* marry Addison, but well, hell, he didn't want to plan that far out.

"I've been off course for most of the year," he said, attempting to explain. "Normally, I don't get wrapped up in the thrill of the chase. I don't want to win to say I won. And yet, CEO came up for grabs and that's exactly what I did. Before our trip to Tahoe, I swore to myself I wasn't going to do that again. Not ever. I've been free-falling with you, Addi. It wasn't about landing you and letting you go. I was the one who asked to extend the trip, remember?"

As her eyes flooded with tears, he realized that this wasn't mostly his fault. This was one hundred percent his fault. "And then I asked you to continue once we were home." And then he'd invited her to stay the night again and again. "I didn't mean for you to take this as me wanting more. I'm sorry."

His apology lit her temper on fire. Anger reddened her face. "You never wanted more than sex."

"No!" Hell, that wasn't what he meant. Not really. "Well, sort of. It sounds bad when you say it."

"I've been in love with you since I started working here," she snapped, a fat tear perched on the edges of her eyelashes. "I was in the process of trying to fall out of love with you. But you wouldn't let me compartmentalize after one night in Tahoe. *You* were the one who wanted more, Bran," she added quietly. "You might not have made promises with your words, but your body painted a future with me in it. And now you're telling me I wasn't supposed to fall in love with you? What is it you thought we were doing?"

"I thought I'd finally found someone who understood me." His voice raised an octave. "I wasn't promising you anything. I was living my life one day at a time, which, by the way, is the lesson you should have learned from Joe."

Her head jerked on her neck. A quiet voice warned him not to keep talking. He ignored it.

"If your friend had lived his life to the fullest, he'd have kissed you long and hard, before you knew what was happening. And then you would have told him no and broken his heart. And then—" Bran sighed, hating hurting her. Hating watching that tear tumble out of her eye and knowing there was no way to undo this horrible situation. "You would've had to give him a similar speech to the one I'm giving you now.

"You mean a lot to me, Ad. We work together well here and we are incredible at home—at either of our homes. You're not convenient. You're not a pastime. I still want you. Just not like this."

She shook off his hold, grabbed the watch off his desk and dropped it into his mug of coffee with a *bloop*.

"Fuck you," she added before rushing out of his office.

Shocked and incensed, he grabbed the coffee mug and followed her. "What did you expect? *What?*"

Her eyes darted around behind him but he didn't care who was overhearing him.

"For us to get married and live happily-ever-after?"

"What was *your* plan? For us to have sex and keep our hearts out of it?" she countered.

"I don't want a plan."

She lifted her chin with determination. "No problem. I won't be here to make any plans for you or with you. I quit."

She lifted her laptop and dropped it unceremoniously into the trash can next to her desk, then pulled her purse over her shoulder.

"Have fun running ThomKnox *without a plan*!" she shouted as she stormed by him.

He let her go, growling under his breath and not sure who he was more pissed off with—himself or Addison. Or maybe he could blame Joe. That'd been a good move.

"Dammit, Addi."

He fished his watch from the coffee and dried it off with his tie. It was waterproof. She should have known that. She should've known a lot of things, but she didn't. He'd talked her out of practical, and apparently had fully won her over to his way of thinking.

Because she was in love with him.

But he wasn't denying who he was or what he

wanted—not again. He'd followed someone else's dreams before and where had that gotten him?

This was Addi's dream. She wanted *him* more than anything, or had before he'd turned her down. He was honored. He was floored. But he couldn't say yes, even though saying no meant incinerating the best relationship of his life.

He took one last long look at the engraving on his watch before dropping it into the wastebasket on top of Addison's laptop computer.

If she didn't understand why he'd said no, or appreciate his honesty, then they were better off apart.

Twenty

Addison inhaled deeply, intent on appreciating the scent of her recent purchase. Nothing smelled as heavenly as "new car." Unfortunately that scent also reminded her of Bran's sports car and the trip to Tahoe.

But of course.

She'd spent the weekend car shopping, and while agreeing to a five-year loan wasn't the most intelligent move now that she was jobless, purchasing the car had made her feel better. Or at least more independent.

Anyway, she wasn't broke right away. She had a savings account and she'd been in this exact position before. Each time she'd been out of work, she'd found more work. Although she'd given notice at each of those places and in this case, there was no way she could work through a notice. There was no way she could face Brannon Knox again.

She loved him.

He'd used her.

Things hadn't only ended, they'd ended very badly. There was no recovering from a botched proposal. Apparently, Bran was reserving the love he had to give for a special occasion. And him turning her down had made her feel very *un*special.

Not that it mattered. She was heading to the copy center to print her résumé since she didn't own a printer. All her personal printing was previously done at work.

Soon she'd have a new job—a different job—and before she accepted the job, she was going to make sure her boss was a curmudgeonly, unattractive old guy with no sense of humor. She wasn't going to make the same mistake twice.

Yeah, right. Because you fall in love with all your bosses...

No. Just one.

One she'd wanted to build a life with. She'd talked herself into proposing, so sure that Bran would realize his dream from earlier in the year was meant to be with Addison instead of Taylor. He'd wanted a family—he'd said so himself. Addi wanted a family. They were compatible. They were right for each other.

But she hadn't given him a single moment's warning before she popped the question. What a disaster.

Her cell phone rang from her purse as she pulled onto the highway. Before she could dig through her bag to find it the screen on her dashboard announced the caller's name: Brannon Knox.

She reached for the Decline button as a car nearly swerved into her. She gripped the wheel, moved safely out of the way…and accidentally hit the green Answer button instead.

Shit, shit, shit!

She tried to find the End Call button in between watching the road but didn't succeed.

A second later Bran's voice filled her car. "Addi?"

"Hi. You're on speakerphone. I don't know how to operate this thing."

He offered a dry laugh. "I wondered why you picked up."

She angled for the next exit with the office supply store logo on the sign.

"It's Monday. You should be here. I pulled your laptop out of the trash."

Coming into ThomKnox would only solve one problem. A monetary one.

"I'm not coming back, Brannon."

"Why not?"

"Are you serious?" How could he ask her that? "Because… I mean. Honestly? I'm humiliated."

"Yeah, I can relate. I'm also a member of the recently-rejected club."

"You didn't propose. And you didn't love Taylor. She didn't love you. Your heart wasn't involved, Bran. You said so yourself." Their situation was nothing like Bran and Addi's. Hot tears pooled in her eyes as she pulled into the practically empty parking lot of the office supply store. She parked in the back, her eyes on the big red logo. Maybe they were hiring.

"Marriage is a big step," was all he said.

"I know that. One you were willing to take in order to land a raise but not when the woman you're sleeping with professes her feelings for you. I thought you loved me, too. Obviously, or I never would have asked."

"I know." He sounded miserable. "I'm sorry for bringing up Joe. I was out of line."

"I'm sorry I proposed to you," she said, frustrated by his clinical tone. "It wasn't appropriate work behavior."

"Don't do this, Addison. You have a place here. You belong here. I can't do this without you."

She'd thought something similar when she stormed out on Friday. That she couldn't *live* without him.

Know what she figured out? She could.

It hurt. It hurt like hell and she was going to love him for a long, long time, but pulling herself up by her proverbial bootstraps was nothing new for her. Her parents' love came with strings, and she'd done without their manipulation for years.

"You know, I was fine with a one-night stand." She swiped at the tears running down her cheeks, angry that she was so emotional.

"You were not."

"Don't be a pompous ass."

"You tried to be someone you weren't," he argued. "I recognize that quality well. You were trying to *pretend* you were fine with a one-night stand."

"And what were you doing?"

"Enjoying myself! What the hell is wrong with everyone? Why can't we hang out and work together and have amazing sex?" He lowered his voice like someone might overhear. "Listen. This isn't why I called. I called because I made a mistake."

Her heart—her stupid heart—leaped with hope.

"Remember when I asked you what you were doing for the Fourth of July? I had a plan in mind, but I talked myself out of it. I didn't want anyone to pressure us into becoming something we're not. Come with me to my family's cookout on Saturday. They'd love to see you and you could use the reminder of why you liked it here. Let's fix this. You're an integral part of ThomKnox. I don't want you to work anywhere else."

What a profession! He would love for her to come work with him and his family sure liked her, too. Her heart broke into a thousand pieces hearing the impassioned, incredible man she'd fallen for compartmentalize their relationship so thoroughly.

"And then what?" she asked with a sniff. "Am I allowed to kiss you? To come home with you? To sleep with you?"

"There are no rules. We're taking this a day at a time, not crafting a future everyone else wants. I know why you proposed."

Because she loved him. Duh.

"You feel alone and unloved," he answered for her. "You are not alone. You have me, my family. You have your job. You don't have to orchestrate a wedding to fulfill a need your family failed to supply."

Her tears dried in the heat of her rage.

"You think this was about me not wanting to be

alone?" As she said the words, she only grew angrier. "You think I was filling the hole in my heart with a *marriage*?"

There was a slight pause before Bran said, "Yeah. I do."

"I proposed because I'm in love with you. Because I had a glimpse of a future with you in it." Bran and her and their three children. "You have your head so far up your ass with this 'live in the now' credo that you don't see what's right in front of you! You said there were no rules, but you lied. I broke a very big one when I asked you for more. I won't live another moment feeling way too much for someone who gives me so little. Good-bye, Brannon."

She tapped the End Call button on the screen and stared straight ahead. Outside the window, the giant storefront blurred as she blinked away more tears. They'd probably never end at this rate.

"I won't be told how I feel or what I want. Not by anyone," she said to herself. She refused to feel bad about being transparent. About being herself. She was a treasure. A prize. A goddamn rare find. If he couldn't see that, then the only mistake she'd made was letting him talk her into bed in the first place.

He wanted to live in the now? Well, he was going to have to live with the consequences of not planning for his future.

As for her, she had her own future to plan for. One without him in it.

She blotted her face with a tissue and pressed on some powder. Before she stepped out of her new car, she smiled at her reflection in the rearview mirror. Not great, but it would do.

She was capable of being everything she needed in life. She'd practiced at it enough. This misstep wouldn't slow her down.

Heavy, she trudged into the store, her "you go, girl" speech feeling more and more false with every step.

The truth of the matter was, she wasn't angry at Brannon for not loving her any more than Joe wasn't angry with her for not loving him. She was angry at herself for not reading the signs, for not proceeding with caution, for *not* making a plan.

She should have known better.

From now on, she would.

Twenty-One

Brannon's temporary assistant was sweet, showed up on time and had neat handwriting. She'd also forgotten to remind him about his conference call on Wednesday and he'd missed it. She'd delayed in handing him his messages, and today he'd put off having lunch with an important client until next week to help wade through them.

He missed Addison.

For reasons that far outnumbered professional ones.

"See you, Peg," he said to his new assistant. She was pulling on a light jacket and waved, her desk cluttered and disorganized.

"See you Monday, Mr. Knox."

Not a chance.

He'd have to find another temp in the interim. He'd

made attempts all week to woo Addi back to work. She must have figured out her Bluetooth because he was unsuccessful reaching her on the phone again. He'd had P&P delivered to her front door, had sent flowers and candy and fruit, every one of them arriving with a version of the same note: *Come back to work. We need you.*

If he could talk her into sitting behind her desk again, everything else would work out. He knew it. He couldn't think without her here, let alone examine how he'd been feeling in the week since he'd touched her. Kissed her.

He missed her like crazy.

He wanted her in his bed and in his world. She belonged here. She loved it here. Why was she being so stubborn?

On his way to the elevator, he was intercepted by Royce.

"Are you going straight to the vineyard from here?" Royce asked. "Taylor and I are staying the night."

"That's the plan." Bran didn't feel like celebrating but he didn't want his parents and siblings talking about him. And if he wasn't there—they would. He didn't want anyone worrying about his state of mind or well-being. He was a grown man, dammit.

They stepped inside the elevator and Royce pressed the lobby button. "Is Addi coming?"

"No, she's, uh. Busy." Ignoring him, but still.

"You know no one bought your bullshit excuse about her finding another job, right? You two split up, didn't you?"

"Yes, but it's fixable." Bran had no idea how to fix it,

but he was working on it. She was going to come back. She had to. "We need her here."

Royce remained stoically silent during the short walk from the building to their executive parking spots. "See you there," were the last words his brother spoke before he backed out of the lot and left. Before Bran could follow suit, his sister shouted from behind him.

He turned to find Gia in tall high-heeled shoes jogging after him, a weekender bag in hand. "Can I ride with you? Are you going straight there?"

"Yes, actually. You mean you don't want to carpool with Jayson?"

"Assumptions," she reminded him.

"Get in." He didn't have the energy to argue and she was already climbing into the car anyway.

During the hour-and-a-half drive north, she finally pulled her wireless headphones from her ears and faced him.

"I know the last thing you want to do is talk about it, but for the record I told you Addison was in love with you. You didn't listen."

"Congratulations," he grumbled, turning up the radio.

She turned it off. "Did you really not see a proposal coming?"

"How—how did you…?" How the hell did she know about that?

"The watch," she answered. "I saw it in your lap drawer. I was looking for a sticky note to leave you a message."

"I knew I should have left it in the wastebasket."

"You didn't!"

"Who else knows?" He slid her a glare.

"Come on. You know me. I'm assuming that's the real reason she left? Because she proposed and you said no?"

"You've always been the smart one."

"What a gesture." She smiled softly. "That was really sweet."

"Addison has a huge heart."

"Why'd you say no?"

He chuffed and this time watched her for a beat before watching the road again. "Are you serious? You think I should have agreed to marry her?"

"Why not?" Gia shrugged.

"Uh, hello, my divorced sister. Don't you have a list of reasons why *not* to marry?"

"Jayson and I are different." She waved a hand. "Stop changing the subject. Just because my marriage didn't work out doesn't mean I don't want you and Royce to be happy. Don't you love her?"

"Love is a big word with a lot of bigger consequences, Gia. I don't understand this need to label and define everything. Why can't Addi and I just be together? Be present in the moment?"

"Because, you jackass, being 'in the moment' leads to a future," his sister said as he pulled into their parents' driveway. "People are who they are. You can't cordon off only the parts of them you want. And you shouldn't."

Bran sighed, tired. "All I know is that being around her made me happy."

"Yeah. I know that, too." She touched his hand. "Sorry, bro. It's hard for a lot of people to compartmentalize. Except for me. I handle that like a boss."

"You are the coolest," he said, meaning it.

His mom and dad had hired caterers and the entire open-air patio smelled like grilled meat and veggies. Once the family table was set, Bran lifted his beer to another of his father's toasts.

"My family," Jack said. "I love you all."

Royce sent Bran a bland look that Bran mimicked. Their father so enjoyed grandstanding. While he went on and on about how much he adored the legacy he was building and the great role his family played in it, Bran took a look around the table.

His father and his mother, Macy. Royce and Taylor. Gia and Jayson, even though they weren't together, were sitting next to each other.

If Addison hadn't been so damn stubborn, she could have been a part of this. Isn't that what she claimed she wanted? To be part of a big, loving family? It hadn't been easy for him to call her and offer her a seat at this table tonight, but he'd done it. For her.

Evidently she wanted all or nothing. He didn't understand. Wasn't some better than none? He hadn't landed CEO, and as a result, found that the role of president suited him better. If Addi would open up to the possibility of having some of what she asked for, she could have almost everything she wanted. Sometimes almost was as close as you got.

Frustrated, Bran excused himself from the table, taking his wineglass and half a bottle of cabernet sauvignon with him. He tracked to the stone firepit at the edge of the hill overlooking acres and acres of vineyards.

The sun was waning, the air chilling. He refilled his glass and plopped down in the grass to watch it disappear completely.

"What's up, man?" came Jayson's low voice a minute later.

"I'm not sharing," Bran told him, eyes on the sunset.

"Brought my own." Jayson settled next to him and rested a bottle of wine on the edge of the firepit. It would be a good night to light it. The air was brisk up here.

"What happened, Coop? Did you draw the short straw?" Bran took a swig of wine.

"Are you kidding? No one wants to talk to you when you're moping."

"I'm not moping. I wanted to be alone. There's a difference."

"Yeah, I recognize the difference." Jayson chuckled. "If you haven't noticed, Gia and I have a turbulent but amicable relationship since the divorce. But it took a while to get there."

Bran turned to ask him what his point was, but Jayson was studying the sky.

"Before we could get to the zen state which we find ourselves in now, she and I had to admit how we felt about each other before the divorce. We were in love when we were married. And we had every intention of making it work. After the divorce, we were angry.

Would have been easier to say we never loved each other. In other words, it would have been easier to *lie*."

"Is there a point to this diatribe?"

Jayson turned his head. "If you want Addison back in any capacity, you have to be honest with her."

"Gia told you. I should have known."

"Spouses don't count."

"You're not a spouse."

"I was. I'm grandfathered in. No getting rid of me." He grinned. "Addison proposed and you turned her down."

Thanks, Gia. A whole hell of a lot.

"I was honest with her." Bran could not believe he was explaining this again. "She was on her knees in front of me, pouring her heart out." She told him she loved him. She painted a picture of family and future. She'd been honest and transparent. "I hated telling her no, but I had to tell her the truth. And she hates me for it."

Jayson kept his gaze on the vineyards below, the dark rows and their shadows stretching in the waning light. "Is that why she hates you? Or is it because you lied to her about how you were feeling? Did you take a single second to absorb what she was saying to you?"

It was like his ex-brother-in-law was begging for a fistfight. "Did I take a moment to absorb she was asking me to marry her?"

"Yeah. Did you soak in the professions she dropped at your feet while she was on her knees? Sounds like she was vulnerable, and you were an asshole."

Jaw welded shut, Bran spoke through his teeth. "I'm sure that's the way she saw it. Hence her quitting."

"How *do* you feel about her? Did you feel anything for her at all? Or were you passing the time?"

"I'm not sure why everyone makes that sound like such a bad thing. What is there but time? And we're here on Earth for a relatively short period of it," he said, liking this line of argument. It felt sensible. And making sense felt good. "Maybe I won't wake up tomorrow morning. Maybe this wine's gone bad and I'll die in my sleep." They raised their glasses and took long swigs, tempting fate. "Doesn't it say something that I chose to spend each day with her?"

"Oh, so she should be grateful."

"I was." The honesty of those words shook him. "I was really damn grateful to have her in my life. I learned all these things about her I didn't know. We had a lot more in common than I thought. She sees the Knoxes as some kind of dream family. I don't know, I think she was trying to surround herself with us."

"Are you that unlovable? I doubt she would have proposed unless she was over the moon for you." Jayson narrowed his eyes. "I don't see it. But I know what she means about your family. Why do you think I never left?"

"Maybe she was caught up." Bran shook his head, his mind back on the conversations they'd had. When the night was quiet and their voices were the only sounds in the room. They'd been naked in more ways than one. "I gave her the wrong idea."

"Or the right one. I don't think you've thought it through yet."

"I don't want to marry anyone, Coop."

"But she isn't anyone. She's Addison Abrams. The woman who turned you from an egotistical, hustling boar into a guy I used to hang out with a lot more often."

Bran frowned.

"You were a dick this year." Jayson leveled him with a look.

"Thanks a lot."

"And then you weren't. The right woman can bring out your best. How did she take the no?"

"She was devastated," Bran said before he thought about it. He remembered the acute pain in her eyes when he attempted to let her down easy. Devastated was a great description. "And pissed off."

"Broke her heart. I did that once." Jayson looked over his shoulder at Gia. "What were you thinking when she asked?"

"What do you think I was thinking?" Bran raked a hand through his hair. "I was agonizing over bringing her here. Worried that bringing her to a family event would be putting too much pressure on us. I had no idea she was thinking of—Cooper, what would I do with a wife?"

Using Bran's shoulder as leverage, Jayson stood, his smile evident in the grainy, fading light.

"Love her." Jayson slapped Bran's shoulder. "And hope for the best."

Twenty-Two

After a week of ignoring Bran's repeated attempts to woo her back to work, Addi decided to give her friend Carey a call. One, for emotional support, and two, was Carey's company hiring? Over a lunch at a Mexican restaurant in Palo Alto, Addi learned that no, they weren't hiring. At least she could count on her friend to be there for her emotionally. Carey might well be the only person left.

"I know you're proud, but if you need money…" Carey was saying.

"No, no! That's not why I invited you out. I'm not flat broke." Not yet. Even though the car purchase had put a healthy dent in her savings account.

"I can't believe you quit. You love ThomKnox." Carey's eyes widened. "Oh, no. It's your boss. Who you were sleeping with. He screwed it up, didn't he?"

Addi nodded, swallowing past a lump in her throat. "He did. That's the other reason I wanted to talk to you. You're my person."

Carey's hand landed on hers. "Of course I am! Lay it on me."

All Addi had to do was make it through the story with as few tears as possible. Easy peasy. "The reason I'm not working at ThomKnox any longer is because I quit. And the reason I quit is because I proposed to Brannon Knox." She felt the tears well in her eyes despite her trying to dam them. "He said no."

"Oh, honey."

Addi shared about the watch and the proposal given from her knees. Then she shared that Bran had helped her stand and told her what amounted to *let's forget this ever happened*.

"I don't know if I'm more humiliated that I proposed, or more humiliated that I love him and he feels nothing for me."

"You don't know that."

"I do, actually. He's been texting and sending flowers and P&P takeout."

"That's sweet." Carey cooed, but promptly covered her lips with one hand when Addi shook her head.

"He wants his assistant back. Although I'm sure he would appreciate more sex in the conference room." Addi ate a chip. She was so miserable her taste buds were on strike. It tasted like salted cardboard. "I was caught up," she admitted.

"Babe. *Of course* you were caught up! You were in a relationship."

"Not according to him." According to Bran, they were in a live-in-the-moment sex-a-thon. "Sex changed nothing for him and everything for me. I thought we were building a life."

"You acted from the heart. That's never wrong. It's not your fault he's emotionally crippled." Carey paused to order another margarita for each of them. "Never hold back. Follow your heart. Joe didn't follow his heart, and don't you wish he would've? If you would've told him you didn't want to date him, he would've known how you felt about him."

"Funny, Bran brought up Joe, too. He said if Joe would have confessed how much he loved me, I would have had to turn him down the same way Bran turned me down."

"And Joe would have accepted it *because* he loved you." Carey's mouth twisted to the side. "What a catch twenty-two."

Carey was right. She didn't know Joe, but Addi had told her a lot about him. Addi could easily picture the scene Carey painted. Him telling Addi how much he loved her, and her letting him down gently. He would've joked and said he never expected a yes anyway. He would've let her off the hook.

The same way Bran was trying to let her off the hook now.

The reality hit her with such a suddenness, she felt dizzy.

"Bran doesn't love me," she said as a fresh margarita was set in front of her. "And I'm punishing him because he didn't say yes. That's as unfair as if Joe would've hated me for not loving him back. And he wouldn't have. He *didn't*. He probably kept his feelings to himself to spare mine." Oh, Joe.

It's okay, sweetheart, Joe said in her head.

"Is it better to know or not know?" Addi asked Carey.

"To know."

Carey was right. Addi was better off knowing that Bran didn't want to marry her. She could've gone another year aching for him and waiting for him to ask *her*.

"You know what? I'm going back to work. I can't leave the work I love because he didn't want to marry me. That'd be as bad as him firing me if I didn't sleep with him. Being independent doesn't have to mean burning down every bridge from your past."

Even if it did seem to mean being alone.

She thought of her relationship with her parents and how rough things had been. After she left here, she was going to pay them a visit. What if they'd been reading each other wrong this whole time? What if there was healing around the corner? What if one conversation where no one held back would finally clear the air? And if her parents felt the same way as they always had, that, too, would be an answer.

Knowing *was* better.

"I have the perfect job with an amazing company. And I spent a really great month with a really great guy," Addi said. The silver lining was there, even if it hurt to think about it.

"That's very mature of you." Carey's eyebrows bent with sympathy. "You don't have to be okay right away, you know."

"I'm not." Addi gave her friend a brittle smile. "But I will be. I'm strong. I'm professional. I'm practical." It was her heart that was *im*practical and *un*professional.

If Bran was willing to let the whole proposal thing go and invite her back to work, and after she'd dropped a big F-you at his feet, she'd be crazy not to accept his offer.

She'd been out in the real world, and knew she could find another job. But ThomKnox was more than a job. It was a passion.

So she and Bran weren't going to be married and live happily ever after. That didn't mean she had to forgo her professional future at ThomKnox.

Monday morning, Bran stepped into the office, half expecting Peggy the temp to be there in spite of him canceling her contract last week.

Maybe that's why he wasn't surprised to see someone standing at Addison's desk. But he hadn't expected a trim, beautiful blonde wearing a teal green dress. Her hair was down. Sleek and straight and brushing her shoulders. She turned her head and saw him and he froze in his tracks.

It was the first full breath he'd taken since she left. The first time he felt a sliver of hope that she might not hate him.

"Addi." It wasn't much of a greeting, but he couldn't think of a single other thing to say. He'd been trying to bribe and beg her to come back, and here she was. "What are you doing here?"

She'd told him to fuck off. She'd quit. And the day

he called her to explain himself, he'd been a bigger ass than he had the day she proposed.

She came out from behind the desk and smoothed her hands over her dress. She looked so soft and touchable, and he wanted to touch her. Touch her and reassure her that he didn't mean any of what he said last week, except the part about wanting her to come back.

"Unless you've changed your mind since last week, I would like to resume my position as your executive assistant," she said, her mouth firm. "Maybe in the future I can find another position within ThomKnox, but for now, if you'll agree, I can work with you until you find my replacement."

He didn't want a replacement. At this desk or by his side.

"The point is," she continued, as beautiful and brave as he'd ever seen her, "I can't leave the best job I've ever had. Or the best family I've ever worked for. Are you willing to forget everything that happened and move on?"

Absolutely not. He didn't want to forget it. He wanted to revel in it.

After he'd spoken to Jayson after dinner, Bran had lain in the guest bedroom of his parents' house, wide awake. Anger, frustration and guilt took turns throwing punches until he gave up on sleep and climbed out of bed. He went back outside to sit in the same spot he was in before, but this time, stars dotted the dark sky and the twisting grapevines were gnarled fingers reaching from the ground.

What was he afraid of?

Addison had handed over her heart, so bold, and he'd been a total pussy. And he'd continued trying to stuff her into the limited space he'd reserved for their relationship when they expanded far past it. The sex was fun but it was also so much more. They'd laid out their hearts and dreams to each other. Addi was right when she accused him of making promises with his body. He had.

He'd sat on that patch of grass until the sun rose over the vineyards the next morning. Only then did he stumble inside and make coffee, greeting his siblings and parents with a hazy "good morning." The conclusion he'd come to in those hours alone made him sick and hopeful at the same time.

He'd fallen in love with Addison Abrams, and he hadn't even known it.

He'd decided a long time ago what love looked like but nothing in his immediate world matched the picture in his head. He'd never imagined being proposed to, assuming he'd be the one down on one knee. He'd be the one delivering the big speech and the profession of love.

Addison had ripped the rug from under his feet and he'd fallen on his ass. When she asked him to marry her, he wasn't ready. And what really threw him off was that if she hadn't asked, he might *never* have been ready. If she'd let them continue to be the underdeveloped version of themselves, they could have gone on the way they were for months. *Years.* What a loss that would have been.

As hard as he'd fought against planning anything in life, he'd done it anyway. Not making a decision *was* a decision. Not having a goal was, in its own way, a goal. Declaring that him and Addison were one thing meant they couldn't be more.

"I had a great time with you, Brannon." Her voice was small, tender. Her eyes weren't tear-filled, but they reflected the anguish he knew she'd suffered. "I don't regret it. Not any of it."

It was killing him to see her like this. He wanted to kiss her. Scoop her into his arms and apologize for every dumb thing he'd done since their shared road trip. Tell her that he didn't hold her at fault, but he held her in his heart and wanted nothing more than to hold her in his arms.

"I haven't changed my mind about wanting you," he said, but the moment she frowned, he hurriedly added, "here at work."

Damn. This was hard. It'd taken a lot for her to be so vulnerable with him—so honest. Now that he knew how he felt about her, admitting it was downright terrifying. He could blurt out everything and be shot down, which, arguably, he deserved. She'd bared her heart before and he'd stomped on it.

He swiped his brow, nervous for the first time in a very long time. Facing a live tiger while nude in the jungle would be less frightening.

"Great. I'll just…get started unless anything has changed in the week I've been gone?" She hesitated, giving him an opening, but the timing was off, so he addressed her question.

"Peg probably left you a pile of emails to sort through. And I answered some of them personally."

"You didn't." Addi's lips pulled down at the sides. "I'll have to do damage control."

She was joking. She was here. She was back. It was everything he thought he wanted. Only now that he'd quieted down to give his heart room to talk, he realized he didn't want her like this. He wanted everything she'd give him. He wanted the original vision of him in his head. *He* wanted to be the one to propose. To give a speech. To profess his love for *her*.

The phone on her desk rang and she answered it, lowering into her chair as she did. She hung up a moment later, having already slid back into her efficient pre-sleeping-with-him self.

"Did you want to review your schedule for the week?"

"Actually, there's something I have to do. Can we postpone?" What was a few more minutes when soon, if she agreed, they'd have the rest of their lives?

"No problem."

She began reorganizing her desk and he headed back to his office and shut the door. On his desk sat his watch. He'd had every intention of having the words she'd engraved onto it filed off, and then selling it to the jeweler. Thank God he hadn't.

Now a different impulse came. One that was risky and bold—every bit as brave as what Addison had done.

Or stupid.

He'd nearly proposed once before and narrowly avoided the mistake of his life. But now... He watched out of his window as Addi picked up the phone and held it to her ear. She sent him a professional smile and quickly averted her eyes.

Now he was going to propose to the right woman.

He could only pray that what he had in mind would be enough to win her back. If not…

Well, if not, he'd keep trying. The future mattered as much as the moment. The mistakes made had been his and had brought them here, to a future he *didn't* want.

When she hung up, he pressed the intercom button on his phone.

"Yes?" she answered.

"Let's catch up on what you missed over dinner. I was thinking Pestle & Pepper if that's okay with you?"

"Uh—okay."

"I'll have to meet you there. I have a lot to do today— none of which is on your calendar." What he had to do didn't exist until he'd seen her at the office. Before then, his goal this week had been to try her again on the phone. To text her. To deliver flowers personally and then serenade her from her front stoop if he had to.

Now that he was looking at his watch, he had a better idea. A *bigger* idea. And it'd better work. For both their sakes.

For the future.

For their forever.

She deserved no less.

Twenty-Three

Beautiful girl, you can do hard things.

Like having a professional work dinner with Brannon Knox on her first full workday after she returned to ThomKnox since proposing marriage to him.

Sure thing. No problem.

She was trying desperately to compartmentalize him, and work, and now that she'd entered Pestle & Pepper, she was determined to enjoy her damn self. There was a lot to be grateful for. Whenever she needed to feel loved, all she had to do was step foot into this warmly lit restaurant, be greeted by Mars's infectious smile and order her favorite meal.

As if on cue, the owner, Mars, appeared around the corner like he'd sensed her. Round with heft showing he enjoyed his own cooking a great deal, he embraced her in a bear hug. She hugged him back, reminding herself that red eyes and a snotty nose was no way to greet her friend. Plus, Bran would be here any moment. She refused to let him see her in pieces.

"Your favorite corner booth," Mars said as he walked her to the back of the restaurant. She liked being close to the kitchen, where she could hear the clatter of pans and Mars's big voice. "We've missed you. Brannon Knox has been ordering takeout in your absence. Are you two sharing all those meals he's having delivered?"

A safe assumption, but sadly…

"No." She hated seeing her friend's face droop with worry, so she added, "But he had quite a few of them delivered to me. They were delicious and amazing, of course. I'm meeting him here tonight, by the way. For work."

"For work." Mars sighed and took the seat across from her in the booth. "I'm sorry, love. That's a shame."

"Yes, it is."

Mars nodded solemnly. "I will send out a special dessert for you. You can enjoy it while you wait."

"Oh, that's not necessary."

"You're my best taste-tester," He peered at her over a small pair of wire-framed glasses, his eyes filled with wisdom and love. "It's necessary."

It was nice to have someone care about her this much. Tired of her own melancholy, she said, "I actually do have good news."

"Oh?" Pausing at the end of the table, Mars waited.

"I visited my parents and we had a long, long talk." She'd once told Mars he was like a surrogate father.

When he asked if her father had passed, she said no, and told him a truncated version of her family drama. Since then, he'd proudly referred to himself as Papa Mars. "They want me to be more goal-oriented, but they love me. They're worried about me. They want the best for me."

"They sound like good parents to me." He gripped her shoulder and gave it a squeeze. "Dessert first. I insist."

She nodded and he hustled away.

She'd settled in at ThomKnox with little fanfare today. Other than a visit from Royce and Taylor and later, Gia, the Knoxes welcomed her back like she'd never left. It was a huge blessing. That was the part of her work her parents didn't see. She wanted to be part of a team. She wanted to matter. At ThomKnox, she did. They needed her—even if Bran didn't.

But she couldn't ask for more than he was willing to give. She understood that now. The next time her heart ran away with her brain like the dish with the spoon, she'd first have a conversation with the man she was dating to make sure he loved her *back* before she proposed.

A server delivered a glass of water while she kept an eye on the front door for her boss, a man she used to have dinner with followed by sweaty, delicious, naked time.

She couldn't regret the time she'd spent with him, though. Life was a series of highs and lows, and even if what she and Bran shared was destined to end badly, she'd do it all over again. Loving Bran might well be part of her DNA. There was no removing it, so the only option left was learning to live with it.

"Dessert." Mars settled a small, white ramekin in front of her with the addition of a glass of white wine. "Chocolate mousse with a surprise inside. I can't come up with a name for it, though, so think about it for me, yeah?"

The chocolate dessert was topped with two strawberry slices in the shape of a heart and dusted with a delicate coating of powdered sugar. "It's too pretty to eat."

"Don't tell my guest chef that. This is his first creation. But be honest," he added, his tone low and serious. "Honesty is best."

Mars was staring at her so she nodded her promise. "I will."

Before she could lift her spoon, a figure appeared from the front door. Silhouetted in sunlight, Brannon Knox approached. God, he was beautiful and…wearing a tux?

At the table, he stood over her in, yes, a full tuxedo, his face partially obscured by a black mask. The same outfit he'd worn to the masquerade ball.

"What…are you doing?"

"May I sit?" he asked.

"O-of course." She stared at him, fairly certain he'd lost his mind. A few other patrons at P&P watched him with curious smiles.

"This was better in my head," he said, removing the mask and setting it aside. His tentative smile made her heart leap. She ignored that leap. Her heart had caused enough trouble already.

"This past spring, I learned the hard way you can't make a future happen that isn't meant to be," he said. "I was angling and strategizing for CEO. Plotting. Planning. *Scheming.* I made a lot of mistakes. A lot of very wrong assumptions. I never want to do that again."

She wished he'd stop talking. She wanted to reach over the table and stuff her napkin into his mouth. She'd already come to this conclusion. She'd made a lot of wrong assumptions about him, and about her future, too. If he was trying to explain why he turned down her proposal, she could do without the fanfare.

"You didn't agree to come to the vineyard over Fourth of July weekend, and to be honest, I'm glad you weren't there."

Well. This was just getting better and better.

"Bran—"

"Let me finish." He held out a hand.

She quieted, but didn't know how much more she could take.

"I have been moving forward without ceasing since everything blew up in my face a few months ago. I didn't want my past to catch up with me. I didn't want the future to come, and then you proposed."

She winced.

"I wanted to stop you before you said or did something you'd regret, but I wasn't fast enough. You forced me to turn you down, Ad."

"I know, okay? I know!" She lowered her voice when a couple at the next table turned to stare. "I screwed up.

Just like you. We're the same. Go us. Can we *please* stop talking about this?" she whispered.

His crooked smile flooded her chest with the love she still felt for him. Even being shot down again, she couldn't stop loving him.

"I owe you an apology."

"You don't," she was quick to say. She couldn't let him do this. Every next thing he said was bringing her closer to tears. She didn't want to revisit any of this. "You were right about moving on. When you suggested forgetting what happened."

"I *can't* forget. More important, I don't want to. It took not having you in my arms for me to realize that I fell in love with you, too, Addi. That nauseous sick feeling I had when I was telling you no? That was my gut screaming at me that I was making a mistake. I was losing you in real time and there was no way of stopping it. There is no moving forward without you—not if I ever want to be happy again."

Dumbfounded, she blinked. He—what?

"I'm sorry for ignoring the love right in front of me," he continued. "And I'm sorry for my reaction when you proposed. When you offered me everything and I acted as if it was nothing." He kept those bourbon-colored eyes on hers, regret swimming in their depths. "If you forgive me, I'll spend the rest of my life loving you so hard you'll never feel alone again."

He folded his hands on the table, his tux jacket sleeve sliding up and revealing the Rolex she'd engraved. She stared some more. He waited in silence.

Her brain scrambled to put the puzzle pieces together

between what she believed he'd been thinking and what he'd *actually* been thinking.

Amazing how wrong she could be twice.

"And if I don't forgive you?" she finally managed, because that was really the question, wasn't it? If this was an ultimatum, there had to be a flip side.

"Then you can look forward to ideas a lot stupider than me wearing a tux and masquerade ball mask to dinner, because I'll never stop fighting for you, Ad. Never."

Warmth filled her chest and flooded her face. It was everything she wanted and the man she loved more than anything was offering it to her.

"Part of living in the now is doing what's right in the moment." Bran reached for her spoon and dunked it into the mousse, coming out with a string attached to what looked like...*oh, God.*

He tugged the string until a chocolate-covered ring appeared from the dessert. A ring with a diamond in the center, and it wasn't a small diamond.

He dipped the chocolate-covered jewelry into her water glass and swirled, fishing out the shining, and now clean, platinum diamond ring. With that string, he dangled it in front of her like a pocket watch on a chain. And like she'd been hypnotized, she replayed everything he'd said.

I didn't want the future to come, and then you proposed.

There is no moving forward without you—not if I ever want to be happy again.

I'll spend the rest of my life loving you so hard you'll never feel alone again.

"At least read the inside of the band," he said.

With shaking fingers, she took the ring from his hand. Cold water dripped on her fingers as she tilted the band with the very big diamond centerpiece in the candlelight so that she could read it.

The engraving was one word.

Yes.

"It's what I would have said if I wasn't ignoring my feelings. If I didn't have my head so far up my ass I couldn't see sunlight. I wasn't wrong, Addi. Not about all of it. Life is about being present. But we don't have to let it cost us a future we deserve. The family we both want." He shook his head, a tender smile pulling his mouth. "It's not an accident that you're in my life and I'm in yours."

Tears stung her nose as she continued staring at the ring. Everything she thought she'd lost was being handed to her, and it was almost too much to process.

"I love you, Addison Abrams." Bran stood and then lowered to one knee at her side of the booth. "If your proposal hasn't expired yet, I accept."

Bran only *thought* he knew how Addison felt when she proposed. Now, he *knew.* Knew what it was like to leap without a safety net and risk everything. All the flowers, delivered food and begging in the world wouldn't win her back. Only baring his soul and telling her the truth would. At least he hoped it would.

He was at her mercy. Addison could truly ruin him. Could turn him into a fool if she told him no.

She couldn't tell him no.

She won't.

He was praying and hoping and wishing that she believed him. He loved her. More than anything. He'd been too stubborn to see it sooner. The blinders he wore to protect himself had handicapped him in the end. Now all he could do was kneel before her and hope he wasn't too late. That she didn't instantly write him off. That there was some scrap of love for him still left inside her. That he hadn't destroyed everything they'd built.

She was holding the ring—a good sign—but her face was unreadable. He could hear his own heartbeats, so close together he lost count at four. After what seemed like an eternity, she finally looked at him.

Bright blue eyes lifted her rosy cheeks into the barest hint of a smile. It was like the morning he'd watched the sun rise over the vineyards behind his parents' house. The very moment he'd come to the conclusion that he loved her, and had been loving her the entire time they were together. The moment he'd felt at once free and devastated because he had no idea how to win her back.

His beautiful, brave girl clasped his face with both hands and kissed him solidly on the mouth. He kissed her back, feeling the competing warmth of her lips and the coolness of the metal band of the ring in her grip against his cheek—but mostly relief. So much relief.

He ended the kiss and, before she could rethink her

answer, slipped the ring on her left finger. Clasping both her hands in his, he became aware of the low echo of applause around them and the blur in his eyes from an unshed tear or two of his own. Her next words released them.

"I love you, too." Her grin was wide, her eyes misted over. Then she was kissing him again and damming the words he was going to say in his throat.

That was fine by him. Those four words were the only words he needed to hear until the day they said *I do.*

Epilogue

Addison stood in her wedding gown looking out at the vineyards and mountains beyond. The sun had set, but only just. The sky was a deep navy blue.

"Mrs. Knox," her husband said from behind her, sliding his hands around her waist. Brannon kissed her ear and lower on her neck as she breathed in the clean scent of him.

The night he proposed in the restaurant, they went to his house after and made love in his bedroom. This time each kiss, each touch, each long slide of him inside her was paired with an "I love you." They hadn't spent a night apart since.

It'd been a whirlwind, from their trip to Tahoe until their wedding, with plenty of missteps—with each of them pulling in opposite directions. But somehow they'd ended here, in a beautiful place, after a beautiful ceremony, with another beautiful surprise she'd yet to share...

His parents' vineyard mansion had been packed with family and friends, their "small backyard wedding" a crowd of one hundred and fifty people. Her parents, Joe's parents, and friends new and old were the only guests from her list. Brannon Knox had come with an entourage, but she'd expected no less, she thought with a smile.

Now most of the guests were filtering out to the parking area behind Jack and Macy Knox's vacation home, their cars forming a motorcade down the hill.

Reaching behind her, she stroked her husband's stylishly disheveled hair. "Thank you."

"For?" He placed another kiss on her shoulder and she shivered. She'd come outside, overheated from dancing, but in the night air she realized her off-the-shoulder dress wasn't warm enough to thwart the November chill.

"For being you. For making my dreams come true. For giving me a whole new family in addition to the one I have." She turned and encountered his handsome face, a sight she'd never grow tired of. "I love you."

"I love you." He leaned in to kiss her and she leaned in to accept when a sharp, panicked shriek cut into the air.

They jerked apart and turned toward the patio. Taylor was gripping her very pregnant stomach with one hand and her husband-to-be with the other.

"Here we go," Bran said, gripping Addi's hand and walking with her.

"Someone get those goddamn cars out of the way! *Now*!" Royce shouted, pointing at the parade moving slowly down the hill.

Jack Knox appeared from nowhere like a superhero. "I've got it! I'll take the bike down."

"Dad," Royce warned, but Jack didn't listen, only ran for the garage to extract his new Harley.

Royce sent Bran a look of worry-slash-irritation. "Now we'll have to take him *and* Taylor to the hospital."

"Ohhh, God!" Taylor cried, her face twisted in anguish, her fingers choking the material of Royce's shirt.

Addi ran to support her other side while Royce held onto his fiancée with both arms.

"You two are ready for this," Addi reminded them—but mostly Royce, since he looked like he needed to hear it more. "Bran, honey, why don't you start the car?"

"Got it."

"Oh, Ad. I didn't mean for this to happen on your wedding day. I didn't expect this baby to be a week early!" Taylor hissed another tight breath, sweat coating her brow. "Those doctors swore I'd be on time!"

"Taylor, I'm honored to share your baby's birthday," Addi assured her. "Soon we can finally find out whether I have a niece or a nephew!"

"Right now it feels like an elephant," Taylor growled as Royce shoved a chair underneath her.

"How about an ice-cold washcloth for the ride to the hospital?" Addi offered, and Taylor nodded an enthusiastic yes.

"Make me a gin and tonic while you're in there," Royce said, his tone dry.

Addi laughed to herself—and only once she was in the house. She bypassed Bran's mother, Macy, who was gathering her purse and running for the back door.

"A baby! Oh, Addi, I'm so excited!" Macy squeezed Addi's arm before she darted outside. Addi might be as excited as her mother-in-law about meeting a new member of the family.

Family.

She paused in the hallway en route to the linen closet to appreciate that she had a family. Not only her parents, who had come and gone today already, but a family who *chose* her. The Knoxes had always been supportive and amazing, and now she could claim relation to them. Her dream had come true.

Addi grabbed a washcloth from the linen closet as a door opened at the back of the hall. A sharp whisper that sounded a lot like Gia's said, "You go first! Go!"

Jayson stepped from the bedroom, Gia shoving him with both hands. They froze when they saw Addi and did their best impression of deer in headlights.

Gia's lipstick, if she'd been wearing any, was gone, her lips plump like she'd been recently and thoroughly kissed.

"Addison! Hi! Is Taylor in labor?" Gia smoothed her hair away from her face and grinned, as if a grin would hide that she'd been making out with her ex-husband.

"We heard something." Jayson straightened his shirt but then noticed his zipper was down. He swore and turned his back to close up shop.

Addi couldn't repress her smile at the couple who *used to be* a couple caught *nearly* coupling. Especially since Gia had busted Addi and Bran not so long ago.

"That was Taylor," Addi confirmed. "And yes, she's in labor. She has amazing timing."

"Yeah. Amazing," Jayson mumbled, pushing a hand through his hair.

"I'm taking her a cold cloth."

"I'll do it. You two check on her." Gia took the cloth from Addi, quickly ran it under the sink in the bathroom and then raced outside.

Jayson offered his arm and Addi hooked her hand around it, lifting the edge of her slim, satin wedding gown while she walked. When Gia was out of earshot, he said, "Macy's ceiling fan wasn't working."

"Okay, sure." Addi shot him a grin and he returned it with a smile. She suspected there was more to his smile, and more to finding him and Gia together. Maybe because it was her wedding day and love was all around. Or maybe because she was perceptive. Or maybe, because she liked Gia and Jayson so much, she was hoping with everything she had that they'd end up together again.

"You make a beautiful bride, Addi. I'm happy for you and Bran."

"Thank you, Coop." She rested her hand over his arm. "And thank you for intervening when Bran needed it most."

"He told you about that, huh? Sometimes the best men need a kick to the 'nads. We're not all that bright."

They exited the patio, both laughing as Bran came back to announce the car was ready. "Dad managed to make it down the hill safely and actually moved traffic quite a bit. Need help, Tay?"

Taylor was surrounded on all sides by her mother, Royce and his mother, and now Jayson. "I feel like a parade float with this many handlers. I think I'm good."

"I'll just collect my wife, then." Bran came for Addi, which sent an arrow straight into her heart with Cupid's signature on it. "Hello, gorgeous. Where'd you disappear to?"

"Wait! I'm coming!" Gia shouted as she chased after the group.

"I went in to wet a washcloth for Taylor and found your sister and Jayson, um…preoccupied. He claimed he was fixing a ceiling fan in a back bedroom."

"A ceiling fan," Bran repeated.

"Who knew ceiling fan repair required one to remove his pants?"

"Maybe I should have a look at it." Her husband scooped her against him.

"We have to go to the hospital." She pointed in the direction of Taylor being loaded into an SUV.

"We have time." He kissed her and all reason flew out of her head.

"Lovebirds!" Mars interrupted next. Pestle & Pepper had catered the wedding—their availability the reason they'd chosen this date. "Go be with your brother. Looked like he needed you. I'll lock up and clean up."

"Actually we were going to—" Bran gestured to the house.

"Do just that," she finished for him. She leaned forward and kissed Mars on the cheek. "Thank you for being here."

"Are you kidding? I'm the reason you're married!" He patted Bran's back. "My wife had our first baby twenty minutes after arriving at the hospital. You may not have as much time as you think you do. You kids have fun!" he called as he went back inside.

Somewhat reluctantly, her husband walked her to the car. He opened her door for her as she scooped up the bottom of her white dress.

"It is exciting, a baby, isn't it?" Bran asked.

"It's very exciting." She waited until he rounded the car and was buckled in to share her own news. "Especially since we'll be doing this approximately nine months from now."

The color washed from his face, his finger hovering over the ignition button in his shiny red sports car.

"I'm sorry to say you're going to have to drive something that can hold a car seat. I know how you feel about Red, here." She patted the dashboard. She was sentimental about the car, too, as it was the beginning of her and Bran.

"You're… Are you serious?"

"Telling you about the positive pregnancy test was going to be my wedding present to you tonight. But since we don't know where tonight will take us, I thought I should tell you now."

Gripping the back of her neck, he towed her close and kissed her, taking his time which was so, so precious considering the circumstances.

"What was that for?" she whispered as Royce started down the hill, honking the horn.

"You've given me everything I've ever wanted," Bran said, never taking his eyes off her.

She kissed him once more, knowing the clock was ticking but unable to resist. "You started it."

* * * * *

Don't miss Gia's story in
the final Kiss and Tell novel
One Reckless Kiss
Available July 2020!

WE HOPE YOU ENJOYED
THIS BOOK FROM

⬧ HARLEQUIN
DESIRE

*Luxury, scandal, desire—welcome to
the lives of the American elite.*

Be transported to the worlds of oil barons, family dynasties,
moguls and celebrities. Get ready for juicy plot twists,
delicious sensuality and intriguing scandal.

6 NEW BOOKS AVAILABLE EVERY MONTH!

COMING NEXT MONTH FROM

DESIRE

Available May 5, 2020

#2731 CLAIMED BY A STEELE
Forged of Steele • by Brenda Jackson
When it comes to settling down, playboy CEO Gannon Steele has a ten-year plan. And it doesn't include journalist Delphine Ryland. So why is he inviting her on a cross-country trip? Especially since their red-hot attraction threatens to do away with all his good intentions...

#2732 HER TEXAS RENEGADE
Texas Cattleman's Club: Inheritance • by Joanne Rock
When wealthy widow and business owner Miranda Dupree needs a security expert, there's only one person for the job—her ex, bad boy hacker Kai Maddox. It's all business until passions reignite, but will her old flame burn her a second time?

#2733 RUTHLESS PRIDE
Dynasties: Seven Sins • by Naima Simone
Putting family first, CEO Joshua Lowell abandoned his dreams to save his father's empire. When journalist Sophie Armstrong uncovers a shocking secret, he'll do everything in his power to shield his family from another scandal. But wanting her is a complication he didn't foresee...

#2734 SCANDALOUS REUNION
Lockwood Lightning • by Jules Bennett
Financially blackmailed attorney Maty Taylor must persuade her ex, Sam Hawkins, to sell his beloved distillery to his enemy. His refusal does nothing to quiet the passion between Maty and Sam. When powerful secrets are revealed, can their second chance survive?

#2735 AFTER HOURS SEDUCTION
The Men of Stone River • by Janice Maynard
When billionaire CEO Quinten Stone is injured, he reluctantly accepts live-in help at his remote home from assistant Katie Duncan—who he had a passionate affair with years earlier. Soon he's fighting his desire for the off-limits beauty as secrets from their past resurface...

#2736 SECRETS OF A FAKE FIANCÉE
The Stewart Heirs • by Yahrah St. John
Rejected by the family she wants to know, Morgan Stewart accepts Jared Robinson's proposal to pose as his fiancée to appease his own family. But when their fake engagement uncovers real passion, can Morgan have what she's always wanted, or will a vicious rumor derail everything?

SPECIAL EXCERPT FROM

⬧ HARLEQUIN

DESIRE

Putting family first, CEO Joshua Lowell abandoned his dreams to save his father's empire. When journalist Sophie Armstrong uncovers a shocking secret, he'll do everything in his power to shield his family and his pride from another scandal. But wanting her is a complication he didn't foresee…

Read on for a sneak peek at
Ruthless Pride
by USA TODAY *bestselling author Naima Simone*

"Stalking me, Ms. Armstrong?" he drawled, his fingers gripping his water bottle so tight, the plastic squeaked in protest.

He immediately loosened his hold. Damn, he'd learned long ago to never betray any weakness of emotion. People were like sharks scenting bloody chum in the water when they sensed a chink in his armor. But when in this woman's presence, his emotions seemed to leak through like a sieve. The impenetrable shield barricading him that had been forged in the fires of pain, loss and humiliation came away dented and scratched after an encounter with Sophie. And that presented as much of a threat, a danger to him, as her insatiable need to prove that he was a deadbeat father and puppet to a master thief.

"Stalking you?" she scoffed, bending down to swipe her own bottle of water and a towel off the ground. "Need I remind you, it was you who showed up at my job yesterday, not the other way around. So I guess that makes us even in the showing-up-where-we're-not-wanted department."

"Oh, we're not even close to anything that resembles even, Sophie," he said, using her name for the first time aloud. And damn if it didn't taste good on his tongue. If he didn't sound as if he were stroking the two syllables like they were bare, damp flesh.

"I hate to disappoint you and your dreams of narcissistic grandeur, but I've been a member of this gym for years." She swiped her towel over her throat and upper chest. "I've seen you here, but it's not my fault if you've never noticed me."

"That's bull," he snapped. "I would've noticed you."

The words echoed between them, the meaning in them pulsing like a thick, heavy heartbeat in the sudden silence that cocooned them. Her silver eyes flared wide before they flashed with…what? Surprise? Irritation? Desire. A liquid slide of lust prowled through him like a hungry—so goddamn hungry—beast.

The air simmered around them. How could no one else see it shimmer in waves from the concrete floor like steam from a sidewalk after a summer storm?

She was the first to break the visual connection, and when she ducked her head to pat her arms down, the loss of her eyes reverberated in his chest like a physical snapping of tautly strung wire. He fisted his fingers at his side, refusing to rub the echo of soreness there.

"Do you want me to pull out my membership card to prove that I'm not some kind of stalker?" She tilted her head to the side. "I'm dedicated to my job, but I refuse to cross the line into creepy…or criminal."

He ground his teeth against the apology that shoved at his throat, but after a moment, he jerked his head down in an abrupt nod. "I'm sorry. I shouldn't have jumped to conclusions." And then because he couldn't resist, because it still gnawed at him when he shouldn't have cared what she—a reporter—thought of him or not, he added, "That predilection seems to be in the air."

She narrowed her eyes on him, and a tiny muscle ticked along her delicate but stubborn jaw. Why that sign of temper and forced control fascinated him, he opted not to dwell on. "And what is that supposed to mean?" she asked, the pleasant tone belied by the anger brewing in her eyes like gray storm clouds.

Moments earlier, he'd wondered if fury or desire had heated her gaze.

God help him, because masochistic fool that he'd suddenly become, he craved them both.

He wanted her rage, her passion…wanted both to beat at him, heat his skin, touch him. Make him feel.

Mentally, he scrambled away from that, that need, like it'd reared up and flashed its fangs at him. The other man he'd been—the man who'd lost himself in passion, paint and life captured on film—had drowned in emotion. Willingly. Joyfully. And when it'd been snatched away—when that passion, that life—had been stolen from him by cold, brutal reality, he'd nearly crumbled under the loss, the darkness. Hunger, wanting something so desperately, led only to the pain of eventually losing it.

He'd survived that loss once. Even though it'd been like sawing off his own limbs. He might be an emotional amputee, but dammit, he'd endured. He'd saved his family, their reputation and their business. But he'd managed it by never allowing himself to need again.

And Sophie Armstrong, with her pixie face and warrior spirit, wouldn't undo all that he'd fought and silently screamed to build.

Don't miss what happens next in…
Ruthless Pride *by Naima Simone,*
the first in the Dynasties: Seven Sins series,
where passion may be the only path to redemption.

Available May 2020 wherever
Harlequin Desire books and ebooks are sold.

Harlequin.com

Love Harlequin romance?

DISCOVER.

Be the first to find out about promotions,
news and exclusive content!

Facebook.com/HarlequinBooks

Twitter.com/HarlequinBooks

Instagram.com/HarlequinBooks

Pinterest.com/HarlequinBooks

ReaderService.com

EXPLORE.

Sign up for the Harlequin e-newsletter and
download a free book from any series at
TryHarlequin.com

CONNECT.

Join our Harlequin community to
share your thoughts and connect
with other romance readers!
Facebook.com/groups/HarlequinConnection

HSOCIAL2020

2/13/22
10